BRIDGE MY WAY

Zia Mahmood, recently voted the World's Bridge Personality of the Decade by *International Popular Bridge Monthly* in the UK and by *Bridge Today* in the US, is a passionate bridge addict, as well known for his flamboyance and charisma as for his genius at the table.

In the 1981 World Championship he captained the then unknown Pakistan team to the position of runner-up, a feat he repeated in 1986. He has scored an unparalleled number of triumphs in tournaments around the world, including several National American Championships and the $200,000 Omar Sharif Individual Championship. He lives in London and New York.

Bridge My Way

ZIA MAHMOOD

Bridge Consultant and Editor
Phillip Alder

faber and faber
LONDON · BOSTON

First published in 1991
by Faber and Faber Limited
3 Queen Square London WC1N 3AU

Photoset by Parker Typesetting Service, Leicester
Printed in England by Clays Ltd, St Ives plc

A CIP record for this book is available from the British
Library
ISBN 0-571-16721-7

To my mother

Contents

Acknowledgments

First, to the St James Club, Antigua, Michelle, Vivienne and the crab for my most enjoyable stay.

Secondly, to Nael Islam for help in typing up the manuscript. What a way to spend a honeymoon!

To Micki Beenu and Rosita because they'll kill me if I don't mention them.

To Masood Salim, my good friend and partner for twenty years.

To David Burn for his help, especially at the galley-proof stage, and to my publishers.

Last but not least, to Phillip Alder, without whose help this book would never have been ready on time. He gave invaluable assistance in researching material, editing my prose, and in preparing the manuscript for the publisher.

1

Falling in Love

One million pounds . . . that's the largest bet I've ever made. You might think that makes me a big-time gambler. Not at all – just a bridge player.

You see, I wasn't taking a crazy risk when I made the bet, which was that no one could write a computer program to beat me at the game of bridge. I was betting on a sure thing.

The world has an idea that bridge is a mathematical game, and that you need a computer-type mind to enjoy it and play it well. The world is wrong as usual. The people who actually play bridge know better, and that is why this challenge, made on national TV in England, apparently so full of bravado, was never taken up. It did, however, attract a few interesting letters to the BBC, like the following:

> Dear Sir
>
> For some time I have been following Mr Mahmood around the Tournament Circuit without him knowing it. I am almost ready to take up the bet, but need a small amount of assistance to finish my research. Would an advance of £20,000 be possible? Can you help? Thank you.

Another:

> Dear Sir
>
> I could easily arrange to invent a computer program to beat Mr Mahmood and win the £1,000,000. However, I am slightly inconvenienced at the moment as I am serving a fifteen-year jail sentence for murder. If you could arrange an early parole, I am sure I would be happy to take up and win the bet.

The Weasel burst in, interrupting my story. 'Zia you must have been nuts; you were absolutely crazy! Everybody knows that computers can't play bridge. Even my daughter could have won that bet, and she's only nine years old.' Paul Trent, known affectionately as the Weasel, is a tough, professional bridge player from New York who plays for high stakes. I'm not sure how he got the name, but I've a suspicion it's partly because he plays the cards with incredible speed, dexterously slipping in and out of dangerous contracts. Also, with his small frame and sharp features, he looks a lot like a weasel.

It was early afternoon, Sunday 6 May 1990, and the Weasel was one of three people in a car that was speeding away from the muggers and madness of New York. We were heading to the normally avoidable, but for once very inviting, gambling town of Atlantic City.

I say avoidable because to anyone who has experienced the style of the more elegant casinos of Europe, Atlantic City is a horror. The better-known Las Vegas has some atmosphere; Atlantic City has none.

Forget the James Bond image of beautiful people dressed in perfectly cut evening clothes sipping champagne. Think instead of fat, sweaty people with buckets full of coins and a uniform of tee-shirt, shorts and sneakers.

Forget the thoughts of emotionless elegance while a player cooly wins a fortune on the baccarat table. Picture instead a yelp and an 'All right, you sucker!' as a taxi-driver from New Jersey wins seven dollars in quarters from a one-armed bandit, and celebrates with a hot-dog.

To be fair, Las Vegas has some great shows; cabarets performed by really excellent entertainers. Even Atlantic City has the occasional super-star; but the quality sinks rapidly in anything except these shows.

'Not so crazy. If you're going to make a bet that large, there's no harm in having the odds stacked in your favour.' This came from Tim 'Mr Backgammon' Holland. Well dressed and well travelled, Tim is a talented guy: an expert's expert at backgammon, golf and bridge. And he knows about making bets; he has been making them for most of his life. Considering his large number of ex-wives and his even larger alimony payments, I have a feeling those bets have been more than slightly successful.

We were headed to the S— Hotel, where on Monday we would sit down at the tables and take part in the most lucrative bridge tournament ever held: the Omar Sharif Individual World Championship. From a total purse of $200,000, the first prize was a juicy $40,000.

More than 200 bridge players from all over the world would be coming to the city. Most of them would be sharp-witted and skilful; all of them would be hungry for victory.

It reminded me a bit of an old Western, where all the best gunslingers were riding into town for a shoot-out to find out who was the fastest.

'How do you rate your chances, Zia?' Tim continued. 'You know you must be one of the favourites.'

I was about to protest indignantly that in an event like this it was impossible to have a favourite. There were too many good players, too many imponderables. No one would play with his regular partner; you would play with someone different every round, someone you had probably never even played with before. It would be a lottery.

But I reverted to type when I answered, 'I feel good, Tim. I'm going to win.'

If you're about to fight a war, you'd better not think about losing. And, returning to my earlier gunslinger analogy, I *was* the fastest, I *was* the best, and when the dust had settled in four days' time, I had every intention of being the last one standing, guns smoking victorious. I wanted to win, not just for the money, although this was certainly attractive, but mostly because the winner would earn the undisputed right to be called the best individual bridge player in the world.

I deserved that right.

Do you remember Edward G. Robinson in *The Cincinnati Kid?* Well, today I was The Man. It was *my* game. It had taken me a long time to earn this position, but today it was mine, and no fresh kid was going to get lucky and take it away from me.

A long time, I said. In fact it had been almost twenty years. Looking back, it seems strange to think about the years when I didn't play bridge. How *does* someone become a full-time bridge player? Become that rare animal, something between an artist and a hustler who wanders the world like a nomad, looking for the next game, searching constantly yet forlornly for the elusive perfect hand?

I was born in Pakistan, into one of the powerful 'Twenty Families', as they are called. The men were traditionally expected to become businessmen or politicians, and the children had marriages arranged by their parents: a system that somehow worked then – and still works remarkably successfully today.

My father died in a plane crash when I was very young. One of the few things found in the wreckage was his briefcase. Inside was a sheet of paper detailing all his assets. It seems that when he realized that the plane was going to crash, he wrote them all down on paper, then carefully locked the sheets in his briefcase.

My mother was a remarkable woman who was a rebel by the standards of the day. In a strongly Muslim country where women usually stay at home and raise families, she became a gynaecologist – at that time, a move almost unheard of for a woman. She would administer to the wealthy and the poor alike. The only difference was that she charged the wealthy, using those fees to subsidize her treatment of the poor.

When my father died, my mother decided that she would move to England to further her career. Another good reason for this move was to give my brother and myself an English education, much favoured at the time in Pakistan. We were sent to the very British Rugby Public School.

I did well and enjoyed sports but hated the traditions and rules. I couldn't see the logic in not being permitted to carry an umbrella in the rain, or why healthy young boys weren't allowed to mix with healthy young girls. I studied foreign languages, not the higher mathematics that, according to popular misconception, bridge players need.

However, I suppose I must admit that I enjoyed the experience as a whole, and I can thank the school for two tangible advantages that have affected my life.

First, several years later my brother was sent to jail in Pakistan for being in the opposition political party. Unlike in Britain, our system was not such that you could stand on a soapbox at Hyde Park Corner and criticize the government; if you tried to air your views, the soapbox was likely to be shot at – and you along with it.

My brother was kept in prison for a year, part of the time in solitary confinement – a frightening ordeal. Regularly, he heard fellow prisoners being beaten, and he had scorpions (without their stings, though he didn't know it at the time) thrown into his cell.

Altogether a rather harrowing experience, you might think. Apparently not. When the case was finally thrown out by the Supreme Court as having been fabricated, my brother's first comment upon being released from jail was, 'Thank God for Rugby. After that, jail was almost comfortable!'

Second, I carried out some extra-curricular research during my time at Rugby. An extract from Peter Ustinov's hilarious book *Dear Me* accurately describes the level of sex education: 'An old friend, inventor Sir Clifford Norton, told me about sex education at Ruby before the First World War. The headmaster, who must have been an enlightened man, summoned all the boys who had reached the age of puberty to his study and, after reassuring himself that the door was finally secured, made the following brief announcement, "If you touch it, it will fall off".' I was once even admonished for going out with a girl. I was told it was natural at that age to like boys, but that girls were forbidden!

In our final term, the leavers were addressed by the Headmaster. He gave us a talk about the outside world and life. For most of us, this was too late, as we were already well down the road to ruin. But he did say one thing that has stuck in my mind. 'Some time in your life you'll come to a moment when you will ask yourself the question. "Should I get married to so-and-so?" When that time comes, my advice is *don't* get married. But if ever a day comes when you think to yourself, "I *must* get married to so-and-so, I can't wait," that's the time. You've found the right person.'

I'm not sure whether I should blame him or thank him, but the advice still sounds good. I was a bachelor then and I happily remain one today.

At seventeen I had the choice of staying on at Rugby, with the intention of trying for a place at Oxford, or leaving immediately for the temptations and flesh-pots of London. I chose London.

I eventually decided to become a chartered accountant. I was to find that it is the only profession with a more boring image than bridge.

Even, so, I joined an accounting firm in the City, and launched myself into the London of the Swinging Sixties. Carnaby Street was full of colour; new dance crazes appeared almost daily; the Beatles and Rolling Stones were idolized; the night-clubs were buzzing.

Almost overnight clothes were metamorphosed from stark to sexy. I remember struggling bleary-eyed into work one morning and seeing my friend and fellow trainee David smiling all over his face. David was a great guy, but happened to be Jewish, Indian and a dwarf! Luckily, he had a terrific sense of humour. I was in a foul mood, having lost in a casino the night before. 'David,' I said, 'you're Jewish, Indian and a dwarf – what have you got to be so happy about?'

His grin grew even wider as he answered. 'Somebody called Mary Quant just invented the mini-skirt. How would you feel if you were as short as me?'

This was the age of free love, flower power and long hair. It was impossible not to be caught up in the atmosphere. I wasn't exactly a hippie, but nobody would have said I was the conventional city type either. With due respect to the British city image, it was and is far removed from my style. This sometimes caused me problems. I remember a partner at my very conservative accounting firm telling me to get my hair cut. Naturally, I arrived late for work the next morning, having been to the barber.

'Why did you have your hair cut in office time?'

'It grows in office time.'

'It doesn't all grow in office time.'

'I didn't have it all cut off.'

That was either nimble repartee or too much *chutzpah*, depending on where you come from.

I suppose it wasn't surprising that I was soon fired from this particular firm. I found ticking ledgers and other routine work exceedingly boring, and spent as much time as possible enjoying life. For me, this meant playing cards and pursuing women. Not long after, though, I joined a much smaller, less traditional accounting firm. There was an existing staff of three, I made it four. The one and only partner was the treasurer of Hendon Dog Track. He was a man after my own heart, and I found working there much more my style.

The distractions were not good for my career advancement, and I failed the exams comfortably the first time. But I wasn't worried; in the sixties it was easy to be happy. I was having a great time, and bridge was the furthest thing from my mind. Cards, on the other hand, I did find interesting – though I played only poker and blackjack. For a time I even moonlighted as a croupier in a poker club. There I met some of the more interesting – and more dangerous – members of the London club world. One of them was Lucky Gordon, of Christine Keeler fame, who sang songs like Nat King Cole while taking my money at rummy like Al Capone.

Another, a neanderthal called Man Mountain, lost heavily one evening. Being of a rather primitive mind, he took out his frustrations by almost destroying the club and the people in it, including me. I found that a convincing argument for staying away from the world of gambling. It was some time before I returned to the tables, concentrating instead on my studies.

After somehow managing to pass the exams the second time around, I found myself a qualified accountant. I was twenty-two years old. Almost immediately afterwards my mother died suddenly. So I returned home to Pakistan where, for a while, I did what I was trained to do – work. I ran the family newspaper business.

In marked contrast to London in the sixties the social scene for the young in Pakistan was limited, girls traditionally being kept at home until marriage. At the time, I was trying to get better acquainted with an attractive young woman whom I knew only slightly. The good news was that she finally agreed to meet me. The bad news was that the venue was a bridge party. It wasn't my idea of a perfect date as I couldn't even play bridge, but it was better than nothing.

I had, of course, told my date that I could play. To avoid looking too foolish, I picked up a book, Alfred Sheinwold's *Five Weeks to Winning Bridge*. I hoped I could compress those five weeks into just three days. Much to my surprise, I found the book interesting.

The big day arrived and, as you can imagine, I performed embarrassingly badly – though I just about managed to save myself from complete exposure. But I was sufficiently intrigued by the game that my concentration was diverted from the girl – my reason for being there in the first place – to the intricacies of the game itself.

That was almost the last I saw of her. I became enthralled; the spark had been lit, and soon became a fire. No, not a fire, more like a furnace. Over the next few months I read all the bridge books I could lay my hands on. My intention was to learn the rules and techniques, but through their pages I was also introduced to the fascinating people inhabiting the world of bridge. People like the showman Ely Culbertson, who had promoted the game by his eccentric behaviour, extravagant boasts and famous challenge matches. He had been to bridge what Cassius Clay was to boxing.

I read of the remarkable feats of the invincible Italian Blue Team, the Squadra Azzurra. Its heroes – Benito Garozzo, Giorgio Belladonna and Pietro Forquet – had monopolized world bridge for years and I marvelled at the genius of their play.

I learned how Ira Corn, a Texas millionaire and bridge fanatic, resolved to bring the World Championship back to America. He hired a team of the best professionals, housed them in Dallas, gave them a coach (a retired army man), and made them train full time, like soldiers, to be physically and mentally prepared to win. His strategy worked, the team, the Aces, succeeding in 1970.

At that time, it never occurred to me that many of these people would become my friends, some even my partners.

Two books stick vividly in my mind. *Right Through the Pack*, by Robert Darvas and Norman de Villiers Hart, a charming fairy-tale collection of bridge hands; and Terence Reese's *Play Bridge with Reese*. I have read both of them many times, and recommend them unreservedly.

Hooked, I started to play daily with a group of friends. Like all beginners, I experienced mostly frustration. I would finally master one point, only to find that there were many others to learn and conquer. But I remember the pleasure, the mixture of pride and satisfaction, after making a good play – a feeling no non-bridge player can understand.

When I take an interest in something I become a fanatic. I can't help it; I become totally obsessed. I was determined not just to learn the game but to master it and become an expert player. I was in a hurry, too, which didn't help. But learning was such fun that the time flew by painlessly, and I started to get better.

Non-bridge players, scared of taking up the game, always protest, 'I'm sure you must be very good with numbers!' or, 'You must have started when you were very young.' Neither could be further from the truth. You might need to be able to count to thirteen – which most people have been able to do since they were two or three years old. The only tough calculation I ever have to make is after the game, when I add up how much money I've won or lost on the day. So much for arithmetic.

I started to learn the game aged twenty-four. I had never even thought about bridge before that. If you have a talent or just an interest, age isn't that important. Having mentioned talent, it is interesting to speculate about just what qualities or talents are required by a bridge player. Which type of person does well at the game?

Those are tough questions to answer. To try to uncover the truth, I asked fifty of the world's best players to give me one word to describe a top bridge player. What did I find out? Nothing! Or, more accurately, the answers varied so much that it appears nobody has any real idea. Here are some of the words they came up with: imagination, intensity, concentration, talent, judgment, stamina, logic, focused, aware, card-sense, desire to win, technique, determination, creativity, quickness of thought, discipline, dedication, consistency, psychology, relaxed, confident. In other words, anything and everything. I don't think there is anyone who wouldn't identify with at least one of these words, probably with several. Still, it is interesting to note that not one person mentioned mathematics in any shape or form.

The truth is that the best players have greatly varied personalities and characteristics. All sorts of people can succeed in bridge; there is no stereotype for the perfect player, and every player will emphasize the importance of different qualities. For my part, I think the three most important talents are a logical and clear-thinking mind, card-sense, and a positive mental attitude. Ideally, a mixture of Solomon, Nick the Greek and Muhammad Ali.

There is one more thing, a trait rather than a talent, I have found that most top players have enormous egos. I am no exception in this respect, indeed, am sometimes cited as one of the worst offenders! My excuse, if I need one, is that it's necessary to remain strong and confident in one's own ability. It is easier to win when you are the best – or when at least think you are.

Someone once asked the American player Bob Hamman, one of the greatest players of all time and a good friend, if he thought anybody else played as well as he does. He thought it over for a moment and then replied, 'Maybe God – on a good day!' I think he was just being modest . . .

Anyway, after about six months of fanatical playing and reading, of regularly falling asleep at work, and of being ostracized and abused by non-bridge-playing friends, things were getting better. I can still recall the afternoon when I played a hand that reduced to this three-card ending:

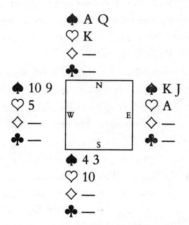

As South, and needing to win two out of the three tricks to make the contract, I was just about to take the spade finesse when somewhere a light dawned. Instead I led the ten of hearts, endplaying East to lead away from the king of spades. Looking back now, it's no big deal. But at the time I was euphoric. I relived the play in my mind time and again, and couldn't wait for another chance to execute an endplay. I suppose that was the point of no return. From that moment the game had me; I was addicted.

It was here that fate intervened. It was 1975 and the Oil Boom in the Middle East had just begun. The feeling in the oil-rich countries was like that during the Klondike Gold Rush – with fortunes waiting to be made.

My brother, always the businessman, was disillusioned by Pakistan and his period in jail. He thought it was a good time for us to try our luck elsewhere. So we moved to Abu Dhabi, previously a desert oasis in the Arab Emirates, but then a wealthy country expanding rapidly.

My brother was right. At the end of one year, our business looked as though it would succeed. Despite this, I was reluctant to stay in Abu Dhabi; a year is a long time if it is full of hard work. I was allergic to the regimen, the heat and, most important of all, the lack of bridge. I decided the life wasn't for me.

I had visited bridge clubs on my occasional trips to London, and, though I played for modest stakes, I found that I won far more often than I lost. I itched to get on with playing and learning the game full time.

When I discussed these thoughts with family and friends their reaction ranged from disapproving to horrified. I received comments like, 'People don't play bridge full time.' 'It's just a game; you might as well try tiddlywinks.' 'Stick with the business.'

They say the world is full of willing people – those willing to work, and those willing to let them. I am firmly in the second category.

Being a life-long member of the Black Sheep of the Family Club, if I'm advised to do something, invariably I do the opposite. I decided to roll the dice, catching the next plane to London. I left my share of the business in my brother's more capable hands, telling him to invest it as he saw fit. I took £1,000 with me, £500 for rent and £500 for a stake at the bridge club.

I still remember my brother's parting words: 'If you're going to spend the rest of your life playing a game, then at least become the best.'

2

Better a Live Chicken than
a Dead Duck

Atlantic City, the Cocktail Party

Sunday 6 May, 1990, the S— Hotel was exactly what I expected from a casino hotel – gaudy, glitzy, noisy and thoroughly uninviting. But that didn't matter at all because a bridge tournament can transform any atmosphere. As I walked in, I could almost smell the anticipation and excitement.

At the check-in counters there were long queues of familiar faces – and everyone was in a hurry. We barely had time to check into our rooms and change before the start of the cocktail party that Omar Sharif was hosting for the players. By the time I came downstairs, the party was buzzing. The room was full of bridge players and casino promotion people, the latter smiling effusively and greeting everyone. By financing the tournament, the casino owners were, of course, hoping to make money. They expected that in the evenings after the bridge sessions, the players would frequent the tables and lose enough to make the investment worthwhile.

For those of you who are not familiar with gambling, there is no game played in the casino where the player has the odds in his favour – except at times in blackjack. There, a good player who counts the cards (it is not as difficult as it sounds, although casino staff will hassle you if they realize you are counting) and follows the odds can win over a period. To win at blackjack, read *Beat the Dealer* by Edward Thorpe. The author is a professor at the University of California in Irvine who used a computer to help develop a system for beating the casino at blackjack. He arranged financial backing and subsequently proved his method at the tables in Las Vegas. As a result, casinos changed their rules, but the method still works. Craps allows two of the least unfavourable bets for the knowledgable gambler, but roulette is a quick and enjoyable road to bankruptcy.

The unwritten law in all casinos is: Make sure the 'punter' has no chance in the long run. That's the way it's set up, and it's very successful. If you think that you can beat a casino, forget it. There is no system, there is no formula. Gamble all you like, but only if you are prepared to lose. That way you won't be surprised or disappointed because, believe me, you will lose in the long run.

There was a strong international flavour to the gathering. The majority, of course, were American but there were players from all parts of the globe: Britain, Sweden, Israel, India, Poland, even Russia. But there was only one Pakistani. I was heavily outnumbered, but on reflection I decided that one was all it took to win a tournament.

Bridge is very popular in Poland, and Poles are among the best players. Their popularity is high amongst other players because they come armed with large supplies of caviar and vodka, which they sell to the participants. The dollar works overtime in Poland and the proceeds from sales at bridge tournaments help them to get through the harsh winters in Warsaw.

In England, we have Irish jokes. In America, they have Polish jokes. For example, if an Englishman uses a jump to five notrumps, he is making a conventional, or artificial, bid called the Grand Slam Force. It asks partner to bid seven with two of the top three trump honours. In the Polish Grand Slam Force, so the joke goes, the jump to five notrumps says, 'Hey partner, I've got my two top trump honours. Please bid seven if you've got a good hand.'

If your right-hand opponent opens, say, one spade, and you make a three-spade jump overcall, many experts nowadays play that this announces a solid side suit and asks partner to bid three notrumps with a spade stopper. In Poland, the jump cue-bid says, 'I've got a spade stopper, bid three notrumps if you have a solid suit.'

I was looking around for a waiter when I heard someone shouting, 'Zia, I've got a proposition for you.' I recognized the voice and immediately started to slink away, but before I could move more than a couple of paces, 'Mike' was at my side, pinning me down. Mike is a real New Yorker, quick-witted, brash, and a street fighter. Amusing at times, he knows all the angles and usually manages to end up on the winning side of a bet. Like all survivors, he is a born salesman who could sell a third-hand bicycle to a second-hand car dealer.

His propositions are to be avoided at all costs. I know of at least half a dozen people who have accepted the following 'offer': 'I will give you $100 cash now if you promise to give me all the coins in your pocket whenever I see you.' They soon regretted their folly.

He continued 'I bet you can't give me the correct answer to this little problem.' I was already sure he was right. If someone, anyone, ever comes up to you and starts with this sentence, believe them and don't bet against them – you'll end up a loser.

In *Guys and Dolls*, when Nathan Detroit makes him a proposition, the gambler, Sky-High Masterson, replies, 'When I left home my daddy told me, "One day a man will come up to you and show you a brand new deck of cards, and bet you that the jack of spades will jump out and pour cider in your ear. When that day comes, don't take the bet because you *will* end up with an ear full of cider."' Never take a sucker bet. This sounded like one.

'Mike,' I said, 'I have to see someone. I'll talk to you later.'

It was too late, he had me by the arm.

'Let's make a small bet,' he insisted. 'How about loser commits suicide?'

Typical – only he could think up a bet like that. I almost suggested that the loser murder the other person, but instead said that I would bet one dinner at a restaurant of the winner's choice back in New York.

Happy to have captured his 'audience', Mike relaxed. 'You're a contestant on a quiz show, a kind of *Let's Make a Deal*. You are shown three doors and told there is a Rolls Royce behind one of them and booby prizes behind the others. You choose one. Now the quizmaster, who knows where the Rolls is, must open one of the remaining two doors, one behind which he knows there is a booby prize. Then he offers you the chance to stay with the door you chose or to change to the other unopened door. What should you do?

'Should you stick with your choice, change, or is it a 50–50 guess? Well, what do you think?'

I considered for a moment, almost preferring to lose a dinner and get away than spend ages contemplating the problem. But I hate losing, so I gave it some thought. It seemed to be a 50–50 proposition. I was about to say that when I paused. One thing was for sure – Mike is a devious guy and would never have brought this up if the answer was so obvious. Deciding that betting on the psychology of the individual was better than nothing, I took a chance. 'I change doors,' I said.

I could tell I had got lucky by his hurt expression. But it was only a moment before Mike was back on the offensive. 'You're right; I owe you a dinner. But how did you work it out? Do you know why?' I didn't have the slightest clue but had no intention of admitting it. I did know enough to quit while I was ahead. I smiled knowingly and made a dash for it.

Later, I thought about it carefully and did work out the answer. Here is the reasoning: Let's call the doors A, B and C. In each case we choose A. There are three possibilities:

1 The Rolls Royce is indeed behind A. After we choose A, the quizmaster opens B (or it could have been C which also has a booby prize behind the door) and offers us C. We accept and change our choice. We lose the Rolls Royce.
2 The Rolls Royce is behind B. The quizmaster opens C (he is not allowed to open B this time because the Rolls Royce is there) and offers us B. We accept and win the Rolls Royce.
3 The Rolls Royce is behind C. The quizmaster opens B (he is not allowed to open C) and offers us C. We accept, changing our choice from A to C. We win the Rolls Royce.

As you can see, the odds are actually two to one to change doors. It didn't look like that at first; it is a kind of optical illusion. The argument is like the Principle of Restricted Choice in bridge.

Consider this situation:

Dummy
♠ A J 10 6

Declarer
♠ 8 7 5 4 2

You can afford only one spade loser, but both the king and queen are out. You lead low from hand and finesse the ten. East wins with, say, the king. When you regain the lead in hand, you lead a second low spade towards the dummy. If West plays the last low spade – with the queen still out – do you finesse the jack or play the ace?

The Principle of Restricted Choice states that when an opponent plays a specific card from two that he might have played, it implies he had no choice. Just as when the quizmaster chooses one particular door, it suggests that he had no choice – the other door was not available to him. Here, East had to win with the king earlier because he didn't have the queen. On the second round, you should therefore finesse the jack, not put up the ace.

14

I managed to find Omar and some friends, and we went to dinner compliments of the casino. Naturally Omar had to sign autographs and have his photo taken with various waitresses. As usual, he took it all in his stride, smiling and agreeing patiently to the requests.

As expected, the food turned out to be pretty bad, but the wine was first class. The conversation was mostly about bridge, with one of the Americans arguing with Paul Chemla as to the relative merits of French and American methods. Nobody won the argument, but Chemla took on all the Americans at the table and outshouted them all. The subject finally subsided as we rose to leave the table.

London, 1975

I felt a shiver of fear as Godzilla beckoned me with his long hairy arm. Simultaneously two words rang out across the room: 'Table up!'

'Come and make up the table, Zia,' he growled.

There are more than two million bridge players in Britain, and most of them recognize the familiar cry heard in bridge clubs to signify the end of a rubber. I was in London, at Stefan's Bridge Circle (now vanished), perched above a Wimpy Bar in the Edgware Road. I was eager for my turn to cut in at a 50p table, where I regularly killed my none-too-skilful opponents. There were the usual half-dozen games in progress. The stakes varied from a mere ten pence a point to a not so mere £100 a point. (In London, a point means the 100 points needed for game; unlike in America, where a point is a point. There, ten pence a point would be equivalent to ten pounds a point in Britain). At £100 a point, a rubber can easily cost someone over a thousand pounds. I was still getting better, with my sights set on moving up in stakes as my game improved.

The club was not the most elegant of places – bridge clubs rarely are – but it had its own atmosphere. Like all bridge clubs, its clientele was a real mixture, ranging from businessmen and other professional people who dropped in for a quick game after work, down to the night players and the elite of the gambling underworld. Sprinkled in between were a few housewives, insomniacs and the odd 'professional'.

These were our regulars. Then there was Godzilla.

Have you ever approached a bridge table praying that you don't cut one of the players? Godzilla is that person – and more.

Have you ever seen a game in progress and decided not to cut in because of an unpleasant player still in?

Godzilla is that person – and more.

After the most dreadful results, have you ever wanted to take your partner's throat in your hands and squeeze until his eyes bulged?

I'm beginning to think you must know Godzilla. He is an ape of such proportions that he makes King Kong look like an apology for a primate. He is worse than 'your worst nightmare' – he is *real*.

Away from the bridge table, Godzilla is an amiable, well-mannered, even cultured man, originally of East European extraction. If you sat at the dinner table with him, you could be confident he would select the perfect wines to complement the food, and that his conversation would be lively and entertaining.

But sit him down at the bridge table and something happens – *snap*, he transforms into Godzilla, the most dangerous monster. He makes a holiday in Transylvania with Count Dracula seem inviting.

His bidding is bestial. He uses the Unusual Notrump – normally used to show at least 5–5 in the minors – with four-card suits. He doubles the opponents in a game when they were about to bid a hopeless slam. He doesn't stop bidding a five-card suit until the opponents stamp on him and chop him up into little pieces. His atrocities are legendary and almost beyond belief. Which was his most horrible hand? No one knows for sure, but the consensus is that the following is a strong candidate as the most infamous Godzilla hand:

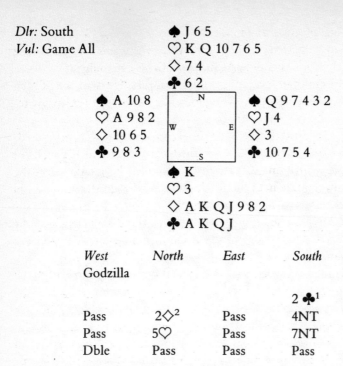

Dlr: South
Vul: Game All

	♠ J 6 5	
	♡ K Q 10 7 6 5	
	◇ 7 4	
	♣ 6 2	

♠ A 10 8		♠ Q 9 7 4 3 2
♡ A 9 8 2		♡ J 4
◇ 10 6 5		◇ 3
♣ 9 8 3		♣ 10 7 5 4

	♠ K	
	♡ 3	
	◇ A K Q J 9 8 2	
	♣ A K Q J	

West	North	East	South
Godzilla			
			2 ♣¹
Pass	2◇²	Pass	4NT
Pass	5♡	Pass	7NT
Dble	Pass	Pass	Pass

¹ Strong, artificial and forcing.
² Negative response; fewer than nine points.

South meant four notrump, as Blackwood, but North thought – correctly, as there had been no suit agreement – it was natural, showing a balanced hand of 28–30 points, and bid his heart suit. South, taking this as indicating two aces, bid a rapid seven notrumps!

Godzilla finally saw a contract he knew he could beat, and doubled.

Godzilla is well read. Nearly every authority tells you to lead fourth-highest from your longest and strongest. So he followed instructions. He led . . . the *two* of hearts!

South played dummy's king, and then ran all his minor-suit winners. At trick twelve, Godzilla had to choose between discarding his ace of spades and his ace of hearts. He looked around vainly for inspiration. He looked for the answer on the ceiling, he searched for it on all the walls, even on the carpet under the table. But finally he guessed wrongly and threw away the ace of spades – seven notrumps doubled and made! No wonder I trembled at his call.

Sunday Evening

Back in Atlantic City, the gamblers prepared to attack the casino tables.

Do you have the impression that bridge players in a tournament go to bed at 9 p.m. to rest properly before the mental exertions of the morrow? Nothing like it. Most bridge players are insomniacs who wake up with a hangover half an hour before game time, which is usually 1 p.m. in America.

Walking into the gaming room, the first thing I noticed was that it was packed with bridge players, who were mostly divided between the blackjack and craps tables. Omar and Chemla gravitated to the craps table, while I decided to check out the blackjack games and looked for the 'right' table. I'm not usually big on superstitions, but there is no point in fighting with Lady Luck. If there is a table where the croupier has been very lucky, systematically beating all the players, it is sensible to try somewhere else.

I soon saw a table where I belonged for at least three reasons. First, a good friend of mine, Alan Sontag, author of *The Bridge Bum,* was already playing there. Sonty has a computer for a brain, and is a card-counting blackjack player. I could let him do the hard work of counting the cards, making smaller or larger bets in synch with him. There were no guarantees of winning but I felt at least I'd be getting the best value for my money.

Second, the croupier – Sarah Jane according to her name tag – was a blonde with a stunning smile: almost pretty enough to make me think I wouldn't mind losing to her.

Third, the table was occupied completely with 'bridgies' who seemed to be enjoying themselves. This meant that they had to be winning. I changed some cash into chips and settled into the game.

The players were knowledgable, hitting on sixteen when the dealer had a seven, eight or nine; and doubling down correctly on nine, ten or eleven when the dealer had a low card. Things started well, and, for a time I joined everyone else in winning. The mentality of a blackjack player is such that he has warm feelings for the croupier as long as he wins. But this changes immediately if he starts losing. This is despite knowing the croupier has no control over the cards being dealt. Casinos don't need to cheat, they win too much to risk it.

Sarah Jane, our croupier, turned out to be friendly, with a sense of humour. While I was winning I promised to send her a present of two racing camels if she kept up the flow of good cards. Not surprisingly, she turned down the camels, but laughingly invited me to make a better offer. I was just about to include a few sheep and an oil-well when the luck started to change. Things went downhill rapidly, so I refrained from making the offer I was sure she couldn't refuse.

Soon, some of the other players gave vent to their frustration. Sarah Jane was sympathetic, well used to this reaction. She kept smiling but kept also her incredible run of luck. She wiped out all our winnings and then some. I took this as a hint that she didn't like camels or sheep, let alone Pakistani bridge players, and I got out of there before she killed me. Round one to Sarah Jane. Loafing around, I passed by a roulette table. Betting on roulette is very unprofessional, but as no one was watching, I slipped a ten-dollar bet on number one, secretly thinking that if it came up, it would be a sign that I would win the tournament. Instead, I saw the ball drop sickeningly into 31. Typical.

It was time to move on once again. Omar's craps table was over-flowing with players and spectators. Omar himself was rolling the dice and at the same time delighting the audience with jokes and stories. Of course nearly everybody bet with him, so each winning roll was met by a simultaneous roar that shook the casino and attracted even more watchers. His bets were very large, the only problem being that he kept buying champagne for the watching ladies when he won, while the croupiers greedily swallowed up his bets when he lost – leaving him not much room for a big win.

Omar made me think of his role as the debonair gambler Nick Arnstein in *Funny Girl,* and I reflected that he probably didn't have to learn any lines. He was a natural. I considered joining the action, but the crowd was too dense. I decided to call it a day instead.

3

Playing the Tables

London, the 1970s

Do you want to start winning immediately? You can!

If I had to give only one lesson to a bridge player – one tip more valuable than any other – it would be an easy task. I wouldn't suggest he learn any advanced techniques such as Key Card Blackwood, Revolving Discards or the Canary Club – the key point is to *play the table*. Forget the difficulties entailed in acquiring the techniques of a great bridge player – *just concentrate on being practical*.

Perhaps at the highest echelon the game does boil down to hair-splitting decisions and expert evaluation. But most people are not at this level. Being practical starts with being aware that each of us is different and your characteristics affect your bridge. The next time you sit at a table, look around and consciously put labels on the players. Is this one strong or weak? A gambler? A mouse? A bully? A coward? Logical? Muddled? If you can do that (it isn't so difficult) and adapt your game to their traits, using their strengths and weaknesses for your benefit, you're almost there.

'Practical' means understanding that your results are often far more likely to be affected by what your partner had for dinner or whether he had a fight with his wife than by the level of his card-play. You should try for the best possible result, not the best result possible.

Forget intra-finesses – think indigestion! If he looks as if he has had his hands on an extra glass of port with dinner, you'd be well advised to take control and keep his hands off the dummy now. That is where the 'money' is made and lost. There is the key.

If you want to be a winner at rubber bridge, remember this lesson. The bottom line is ending up ahead. Forget about the dreamer who said, 'Winning is not as important as taking part.' I'd like him to meet my bank manager and try offering that as an excuse for the overdraft. More to the point is the statement, 'Show me a good loser and I will show you a loser.' Don't let yourself have to show the world what a great loser you are.

However, playing the table isn't as simple as it seems. It is probable that the standard of the players in your game varies enormously. It certainly does in my games. Subconsciously decide in your own mind who is the best player by simply looking forward to cutting him. Similarly, pinpoint the worst player by your silent prayer to avoid him. The next step is to use that information to work for you.

There are two parts to this: the handling of your own partner and the handling of your opponents. Every time you partner someone, even for one rubber, you cease being an individual and become a unit, like a married couple; the winning strategy is to start thinking like one.

You've heard the saying that a chain is only as strong as its weakest link. That saying could have been invented by a bridge player, because a successful partnership is only strong as the weaker partner. Partners must be on the same wavelength, and it is pointless speaking to someone in a language he can't understand.

Suppose you pick up this hand:

$$♠A\ 5\ 4\ 3\ \ ♡K\ 6\ 5\ 4\ \ ◇A\ Q\ J\ 2\ \ ♣2$$

Your partner opens one spade; what would you respond?

No problem, you say, and soon offer your answer. Maybe not to you, but for me this question is vital, not easy at all. In fact, before answering I need to ask a question of my own: 'Who are the other players at the table?'

If you can understand that last sentence, believe it and practise it, you are on the way to becoming a bridge player. You see, almost all the time there is *no one correct bid or play in bridge*. The correct action depends upon the prevalent conditions, and especially on your partner and your opponents. Remember that there is no such thing as an individual action at the table; everything is in the interaction. It is vital to understand this point.

Going back to the hand I just gave you, I could find at least three answers, each eminently correct in different partnerships. If I were partnered with Benito Garozzo, the famous Italian world champion, who loves conventional bids and systems, I would bid four clubs, a splinter bid describing a good hand, trump support and a singleton (or void) in clubs. This bid is descriptive and informative, I know he'd love the bid and, even more importantly, that he'd understand it.

But if I were playing with Rixi Markus, the great British Women's

World Champion, I would respond with a natural two diamonds. Rixi frowns on too much system; her forte is natural bidding. I would describe my hand more slowly, but equally accurately. She would be most upset if I bid four clubs.

Finally, If I held the hand:

$$\spadesuit A\ 5\ 4\ 3 \quad \heartsuit K\ 6\ 5\ 4 \quad \diamondsuit A\ Q\ J\ 2 \quad \clubsuit 2$$

playing with the weakest player in the club, the dreaded Godzilla, I would bid a direct four spades. It would be pointless and foolish to make a bid such as four clubs or two diamonds, which would confuse him (he might pass the former!) and give information to the opponents. Even if he did know what I was doing, he might propel us to a slam that he would be bound to misplay. I prefer to score the game bonus and give up on a possible slam. The only winning method when playing with a monster is to avoid monstrous losses.

In this case bidding four spades, which is the winning bid for the partnership as opposed to the best bid (four clubs or two diamonds), I try to take a plus score. Godzilla may be a weak player, but that's no reason to punish him by giving him a problem he can't solve, or a bid he can't understand. Punishing your partner means punishing yourself. I hope you can see the logic of this argument. A winning player is one who understands the different types of players he is seated with, and then uses their strengths and weaknesses to work for him.

It is like a general employing his forces: as Sun Tzu wrote in his book, *The Art of War*, about the Chinese General, Su-ma Ch'ien, who lived around 100 BC, 'The skilful employer of men will employ the wise man, the brave man, the covetous man and the stupid man. For the wise man delights in establishing his merit, the brave man likes to show his courage in action, the covetous man is quick at seizing advantages and the stupid man has no fear.' Sounds like he played bridge.

A good bridge player employs his forces (partners) too.

Start with a good player. Every game has a best player. Let's call him The King. When you cut The King, put him to work for you. You know he has great skills; use those skills to your advantage. Don't try to impress him with your declarer-play; instead, go out of your way to let him play the hand, or follow his line of defence, and respect his high-level decisions as you do his abilities. Compete fiercely for the partscores; when he is your partner, his judgment will be good and he won't punish you. The best weapon in this partnership's arsenal is his talent, so don't let it be idle – put it to work like a general directing an army. Remember, 'the wise man delights in establishing his merit.'

But things are not the same when you are partnering the weakest player. First, remember that to get the best out of him you need to give him confidence and support. Next, remember that though his bridge game may be faulty, that doesn't make him a lesser human being. You owe him politeness and respect. If you need to attack your partner, wait till he's your opponent – and then 'kill' him on the table with your superior play. But bridge-wise now you are the underdog, so diplomatically yet firmly take over the reins, control the proceedings, even hog the hand if necessary. Be conservative in the bidding, especially when he is going to be declarer. Look for plus scores, and, similarly, settle for a small loss when a dangerous hand is dealt. A weak player made nervous or jittery is twice as dangerous as even his normal self.

There are many tactics to be learnt for successfully Playing the Table. We saw an example above of 'taking the money' when bidding with a bad partner.

Here's one, relating to defence. As you know, good players watch spot cards like hawks, while bad players see things more simply. To them there are big cards and small cards. You can make use of that. Playing with a weak player it's free to false card with small cards. You may lead the good opponent astray and your partner won't even notice what you're up to.

Here is an example of how you can 'break the rules' when playing with a bad partner. It's rubber bridge, you're sitting West, and with neither side vulnerable, you pick up:

♠ K J 3 2 ♡ 7 6 4 ◇ 8 4 3 ♣ 9 6 2

One of these days you'll pick up better cards. Meanwhile, the auction goes:

West	North	East	South
			1NT[1]
Pass	3NT	Pass	Pass
Pass			

[1] 15–17 points

What is your lead?

It certainly looks right to start with a spade, your only four-card unit. But if your partner is one who doesn't pay too close attention, you might try the effect of leading the three rather than the normal two. The aim is to mislead the declarer into thinking that you have five spades.

A suitable layout might find a declarer with this problem:

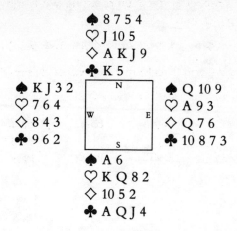

♠ 8 7 5 4
♡ J 10 5
◇ A K J 9
♣ K 5

♠ K J 3 2
♡ 7 6 4
◇ 8 4 3
♣ 9 6 2

♠ Q 10 9
♡ A 9 3
◇ Q 7 6
♣ 10 8 7 3

♠ A 6
♡ K Q 8 2
◇ 10 5 2
♣ A Q J 4

After you have led the three of spades to the queen and your partner has led the ten back, declarer will be afraid that you may have the ace of hearts in addition to your supposed three good spades. He will try the diamond finesse, and will finish one down to avoid giving you the lead. He will think that even if the queen of diamonds is wrong, he will still make the contract if East has the ace of hearts, given that spades are 5–2.

If you had led the two of spades, declarer would have simply knocked out the ace of hearts.

This tactic can be equally effective the other way round, leading the fifth best form, say, ♠ K J 6 3 2.

God Save the Queen

There are many other techniques that are worthy of study. But there are also many *cards* worthy of care.

The queen of trumps is a precious card; learn to look after her.

Everybody knows that declarers take finesses in the play. Very few know that defenders can take finesses in the bidding.

Playing for as high a stake as you can afford, sitting South, you pick up:

♠ A 10 9 8 7 ♡ K 2 ♢ K Q 6 4 ♣ 5 2

The auction races slamward like this:

West	North	East	South
Pass	1 ♣	3 ♡[1]	3 ♠
Pass	4 ♡	Pass	4NT
Pass	5 ♠	Pass	5NT
Pass	6 ♢	Pass	6 ♠
Pass	Pass	Pass	

[1] Pre-emptive overcall showing a seven-card suit and about 6–10 points.

West leads the ten of hearts, and this is what you survey:

Dummy
♠ K J 6 3
♡ A 4
♢ A 5
♣ A J 10 8 3

Declarer
♠ A 10 9 8 7
♡ K 2
♢ K Q 6 4
♣ 5 2

You can see a definite club loser, and there is also a problem in the trump suit which you must solve. You win the heart lead in hand, cash the ace of spades, everybody following, and lead a low spade towards the dummy. When West plays the last low card, do you finesse or rise with the king? How's your nose?

26

While you're thinking about it, try this one. Once again you are in six spades, with the same trump suit:

Dummy

♠ K J 6 3

Declarer

♠ A 10 9 8 7

This time you opened one spade. West, your left-hand opponent (LHO), overcalled two notrumps, the Unusual Notrump, and your partner took over, driving you to the slam. Once again you have a certain side-suit loser and the additional problem of locating the queen of spades. How would you play the trump suit?

I'm sure you finessed West, the partner of the pre-emptor, for the queen in the first example, and East, the partner of the two-notrump bidder, for the queen in the second case. Most people would. Well done – at the table you would have made both hands. Usually the odds would be to put up dummy's king and try to drop the queen. However, following the pre-emptive bid, the odds change making the finesse a more attractive proposition.

But notice how both times a pre-empt signposted the winning line for the declarer. As defenders we all like to create problems whenever possible, but we don't really want to give slams away.

If the declarer is going to play the partner of the pre-emptor for the missing queen, maybe it's time the defence smartened up and started pre-empting with the queen.

For example, non-vulnerable you pick up this hand:

♠ Q 4 ♡ K Q J 10 7 6 ◇ 8 3 2 ♣ 7 5

Your right-hand opponent opens one of a minor. Jump to three hearts. If the opponents play the hand, the queen of spades is likely to be a trick.

However, suppose you hold:

♠ 4 ♡ K Q J 10 7 6 ◇ 8 3 2 ♣ 7 5 2

Try the effect of overcalling one heart rather than two hearts (weak) or three hearts (pre-emptive) which would normally be the bid with the weak hand. Then, the opponents will play *you* for the points. Unless partner has a big hand, you will soon be defending. By making a simple overcall, you will be protecting your partner's key holdings as the declarer will be playing *you* for the missing honour cards.

Similarly, suppose you hold either of these hands:

a ♠ Q 4
  ♡ 6
  ◇ K Q J 10 7
  ♣ K 10 9 6 3

b ♠ 7 4
  ♡ 6
  ◇ K Q J 10 7
  ♣ K 10 9 6 3

If your RHO opens one heart or one spade, I much prefer a two-notrump overcall (unusual) on the first hand than on the second, with which I would simply overcall two diamonds. Protect that queen!

You can protect your partnership's trump holding in other ways. Have you faced this trump suit at the table?

Dummy
♠ K J 9 8

Declarer
♠ A 10 7 6

With no revealing bidding or play, declarer guesses the position of the queen half the time. How can we help him to do worse? Try to give him some rope – just enough to hang himself with. Here's how:

Opening Leads

With something to protect in the trump suit (either length or the queen), make your opening lead as if from a long suit. To declarer, this will imply shortness in the trump suit. Similarly, with shortness in trumps, lead what looks like a short suit, protecting partner's trump stack.

Now for some examples. Sitting West, you pick up:

♠ Q 6 3 ♡ 10 9 2 ◇ 10 8 4 3 ♣ K 8 3

The auction is run-of-the-mill:

West	North	East	South
			1NT[1]
Pass	2 ♣[2]	Pass	2 ♠
Pass	4 ♠	Pass	Pass
Pass			

[1] 15–17 points.
[2] Stayman.

What is your lead? Remember: your aim is to try to protect your queen of trumps.

To imply diamond length, and therefore short trumps, lead the three of diamonds (if playing third- and fifth-best leads), or the four of diamonds if using fourth-best opening salvos. Because of your supposed length in diamonds, declarer will 'know' you have less room★ for three trumps than your partners.

With the same bidding, if you held this hand:

♠ 4 ♡ 9 8 2 ◇ Q 10 8 4 3 ♣ K J 10 2

you should lead the eight or nine of hearts. Let declarer 'know' you have short hearts – and by implication, longer spades. Protect your partner's holdings!

★I am applying the Principle of Empty Spaces. Suppose you as declarer, have to find the queen of spades in the layout above (K J 9 8 opposite A 10 7 6). Unless the bidding has shown otherwise it is 50–50 that (say) West will have Her Majesty. But if from the lead you 'learn' that, for example, West has five diamonds and East three. Now there are only eight empty spaces in West's hand for the key queen, whereas there are ten spaces in East's hand. It has become 5–4 on that East holds the queen of spades.

29

The Singleton Switch

Sometimes fear can be a useful weapon. Before he has drawn trumps, nothing scares declarer more than seeing a defender lead or switch to a singleton. The fear of a threatened ruff will normally cause declarer to draw trumps as quickly as possible, without the luxury of a finesse or safety play. However, what if you haven't been dealt a singleton? You have to make do with what you've been given!

Sitting East, you pick up this hand:

♠ Q 10 7 6   ♡ 10 2   ◇ 9 5 4   ♣ A 10 6 5

The bidding is simple:

West	North	East	South
			1 ♠
Pass	2 ♡	Pass	3 ♠
Pass	4 ♠	Pass	Pass
Pass			

Your partner leads the king of clubs, and this is what you can see after the dummy has been tabled:

Dummy
♠ 5 3
♡ A Q J 7 5
◇ K 7 6
♣ 9 4 3

You
♠ Q 10 7 6
♡ 10 2
◇ 9 5 4
♣ A 10 6 5

The first trick goes king of clubs, three, six, seven. Partner continues with the two of clubs: four, ace, jack. You'd like to make two spade tricks to defeat the contract, but how can you stop declarer from finessing your queen of spades.

Switch to your singleton heart – and quickly!

You don't have a singleton heart? *You* know that, *I* know that, but *declarer* doesn't. If you switch to the two of hearts, South is sure to win in the dummy, then bang down the ace and king of trumps and try to stop you from getting a heart ruff. He'll either curse at you or ask you for a game, depending on his temperament.

This was the full deal:

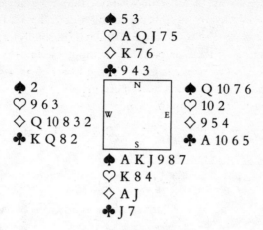

```
                    ♠ 5 3
                    ♡ A Q J 7 5
                    ◇ K 7 6
                    ♣ 9 4 3
   ♠ 2              ┌──N──┐            ♠ Q 10 7 6
   ♡ 9 6 3          │     │            ♡ 10 2
   ◇ Q 10 8 3 2    W│     │E           ◇ 9 5 4
   ♣ K Q 8 2        │     │            ♣ A 10 6 5
                    └──S──┘
                    ♠ A K J 9 8 7
                    ♡ K 8 4
                    ◇ A J
                    ♣ J 7
```

You should realize that if you play a third club, declarer will ruff. Then he will cash one high spade, cross to dummy with a red suit, and finesse the jack of spades, making the contract.

Doubling Cue-Bids
The opponents, on the way to a slam, have thrown in a cue-bid. Often defenders will double the cue-bid to direct the lead. That's as it should be. But, partly because an opponent with undisclosed length in the suit on occasion redoubles and the bid is left in, and partly because it's just the way of the world, the defender who doubled more often than not has length in the suit he's doubled.

As the actress said to the bishop, 'Anything that helps declarer think you're long somewhere will also make him think you're short somewhere else.'

When doubling, don't forget that. The next time the opponents are cue-bidding their way to slam and you're looking at queen-doubleton or queen-to-three of trumps, try doubling one of their cue-bids, regardless of your holding in the suit, and quietly thank me afterwards when you score your queen of trumps.

4

How to be a Winner

Atlantic City, Monday Morning

Today the bridge would begin. People have different ways of preparing for a bridge match. There are those who rise early and go over their system with their partner. There are those who swim or jog, waking up their bodies. One of the players present had cycled for four days to get to the tournament – partly because of superstition and partly to clear his mind. There are even those who take pills, 'pick me ups' and 'pick me downs' – though they usually end up needing somebody else to pick up the pieces. There is another group to which I belong – I sleep. The more I sleep, the happier I am. And the happier I am, the better I play – simple. I like to wake up as close to game time as possible. In my opinion, a tired mind is the most important thing to avoid. You need to be fully alert at every moment. It is one of the facts of bridge life that the one second you spend daydreaming will be the one when you make a mistake.

The only exception to this rule has been my recent interest in golf – a love strong enough to get me up early in the morning. Tim Holland, the golfer, was going to arrange a game for Tuesday. But this was Monday and the bridge game didn't start till 1 p.m, so I slept till noon. I ordered breakfast for 12.30 p.m., and I was in the playing area with a minute to spare.

'How are you feeling,' asked a bleary-eyed Alan Sontag, my blackjack partner from the night before. He added, 'you were smart to leave the game when you did; we all got killed.' Sympathetic, but glad that I had stopped, I grunted something in reply. The inquiry about how I was feeling wasn't just polite conversation. How I was feeling would be important. Playing well and feeling good go hand in hand.

Unlike regular events, where you enter as a pair or a team and play together throughout here we were on our own, each entered as an individual. We would play only one hand in partnership with each of the other players in the field and then switch partners. The challenge would be great but different. Playing well in itself would not be enough. We would have to display adaptability as well as skill.

Let me discuss some of the main problems facing the competitors. Before playing their one deal, each partnership was given one minute to work out their methods. Although the number of permitted conventions was officially limited, this part could be tough. The players came from different countries with different schools of thought and different styles. So agreeing to a common system wasn't easy.

However, I considered it even more important to know to which school my partner belonged. For example, players from Europe, when defending, tend to signal count much more than Americans, who prefer to encourage or discourage, both methods quite different. Not knowing your partner's preference could cost a sackful of points.

Bidding methods, too, vary everywhere, even between the east and west Coasts of America. But rather than worry about individual bidding system preferences, I preferred to know the individual characteristics of my partner. Was he cautious or aggressive? Was he a good declarer or defender? Modern or old-fashioned? Just knowing these things would be a huge advantage. But it was a lot to find out in one minute.

Some players are flexible, happy to play whatever makes their partner feel most comfortable. But others are stubborn, convinced that *their* way of playing is best. They hate to adjust from their type of game. That exactness is fine when playing with a regular partner, but was a disaster here. To win this tournament required a personality closer to the versatility of a chameleon rather than the inflexibilty of a martinet.

I had an advantage in that most people knew me. When I sat down to play, my partners wouldn't try to take charge of the hand in the fear that I was a weak player. This, more often than not, proves unsuccessful, but it would happen frequently to some of the foreign players, even the good ones, who were not known to their American partners. And although a top player's name may be well known, only a few recognize the face. Newspaper and magazine columns always carry bridge hands, rarely photographs.

This is where, I felt, I would have my biggest edge over the field. First, I knew nearly everybody because of my globe-trotting. Second, my years of rubber bridge, learning the hard way how to play with various styles, was by far the best training ground for an event like this – and for winning.

Winning means knowing a few tricks, arming yourself with the weapons of war. First, remember that circumstances change. People vary, and in this field it's necessary at times to improvise, compromise – even fraternize. Over the years I had learnt the unwritten codes of rubber bridge. They would be the formula to follow. Here are my tips for getting the best results.

Partnering the Best Player (The King)

1 Never gloat over good results. Inevitably the better your partnership, the more you will win.
2 Give him the opportunity to put his skills to work, i.e., let him play the hand.
3 Bid soundly so that he can rely on you.
4 Follow his defence whenever you are in any doubt.
5 Double the opponents more often – you can rely on getting the best defence.
6 Overbid in close situations when he is going to play the hand.
7 Don't be intimidated by him. He's your best friend.
8 Don't argue with him. The chances are that he's right.
9 'Pass' the crucial decision to him, especially at high levels, unless you know what to do.
10 Watch him and learn.

Playing with a Bad Partner (Godzilla)

1 Don't give him lessons. If he wanted them, he'd go to a bridge school.
2 Avoid the possibility of accidents: a small profit is better than a big loss. Don't go for the best possible result; the best result possible should be your target.
3 Get an idea of his style, compensating for an over- or underbidder. Are his penalty doubles sound? If so, leave them in.
4 Bid simply; and go out of your way to indicate the right lead.
5 Take control; make the key decisions for him, even when technically this isn't the best approach. Hog the hand
6 Give very loud signals in defence; give him signposts to follow.
7 False-card with the low cards to fool the good player; your partner isn't watching anyway.
8 Protect him from tough opponents, building a fence – even a trap – around him.
9 If you must lose, do it gracefully.
10 Try harder; don't give up just because you're the underdog.

Playing Against the Bad Player (Godzilla)

1 Give him leeway on revokes, bids out of turn, exposed cards. You want to beat him, not murder him – and you have enough advantages already.
2 Never forget that he is going to be your partner in the next rubber.
3 Bad players expect to go down and give up easily, so penalty double at the slightest excuse when he is playing the hand.
4 Allow him to make mistakes: don't get in his way.
5 Understand his style and use it against him. For example, compete more if he doesn't double.
6 Give him high-level decisions. You know he has poor judgment, so let him use it.
7 Play honour cards through him. He'll always cover if he can.
8 Signal as much as you like to your partner when he's declarer: he won't be watching.
9 Keep him on lead, he'll probably find the wrong one.
10 Push him around at the partscore level.

The understanding of yourself is quite as important as any of these tips. It isn't easy to do, but if you can find certain consistencies, strengths or weaknesses in your character, you can accentuate the positive and eliminate, or work around, the negative.

Suppose that you are cautious by nature. The next time you are resolving a close decision, take the aggressive course. In case you have trouble judging yourself (and we all do, if we're honest about it), try this test, which is used on job applicants by a well-known American corporation. Answer each question, and after each answer, give three descriptive adjectives – not physical descriptions like black or white, but emotive illustrations like strong, colourful, and so on.

1 Which is your favourite animal?
2 Which is your second-favourite animal?
3 Which is your favourite bird?
4 Name an expanse of water (anything from a puddle to an ocean).
5 Which kind of drinking glass do you imagine?
6 Which kind of wall do you imagine?

Now judge yourself. Your answers tell you the following:

1 How you would like to be.
2 How the world sees you.
3 What you really are.
4 How you see life.
5 How you see love and sex.
6 How you see death.

This quiz is remarkably accurate. It might not improve your bridge game, but I'm sure you will enjoy the results. Now you know who you are, you have to know how to get the best out of yourself.

To Double or Not To Double

The most underused weapon by good and bad players alike is the penalty double. Not just *under*used, but also *ab*used and *mis*used. In the old days, if Ali Baba wanted riches, he said 'Open Sesame.' Today 'Double' works just as well. It's time to stop playing like a chicken – get out your gun and start doubling.

The first question is: *who* do you double? The answer: *everybody* – good and bad players alike. Let's start with the bad. Remember:

1 Fact number one: the world is overflowing with bad bridge players.
2 Fact number two: bad bridge players love to go down, given the slightest excuse.
3 Fact number three: when doubled, a bad player finds it impossible to think clearly. More, he is so sure that the cards lie badly and that he must now go down, he's almost relieved that he won't be failing in a hand that he should have made.

The second question is: *when* do you double? The answer: whenever the bad player is going to be the declarer and any one of the following exists:

1 Any key suit, *especially* trumps, is breaking badly, particularly when the auction has revealed that they have no extra values.
2 When he's obviously stretching.

West	North	East	South
You			Bad Player
	Pass	Pass	1NT
Pass	2NT	Pass	3NT[1]

West	North	East	South
You			Bad Player
Pass	2 ♠	Pass	3 ♠
Pass	4 ♠		

[1] Made after some thought, which nearly always means he's on the borderline between passing and bidding on.

3 When you want to suggest a lead.
4 You don't like the 'sound' of the bidding – or you just feel mean.

Here is an example from actual play. Sitting East, you pick up this hand:

♠ 7 4 ♡ A J ◇ K 10 9 7 4 ♣ J 9 5 2

The bidding proceeds like this:

West	North	East	South
		You	Bad Player
			Pass
Pass	1 ◇	Pass	1 ♡
Pass	2 ♡	Pass	4 ♡
Pass	Pass	Dble	Pass
Pass	Pass		

The double was based on this thinking: The contract is bound to be close (South is a passed hand, and North bid only two hearts). A spade or club lead may give away a trick – a diamond lead looks best. The more you double, the more you win.

West led the eight of diamonds. This was the full deal:

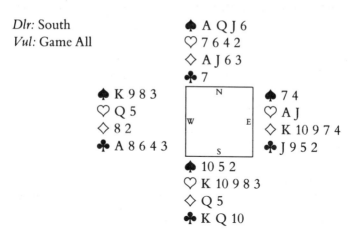

Dlr: South
Vul: Game All

North
♠ A Q J 6
♡ 7 6 4 2
◇ A J 6 3
♣ 7

West
♠ K 9 8 3
♡ Q 5
◇ 8 2
♣ A 8 6 4 3

East
♠ 7 4
♡ A J
◇ K 10 9 7 4
♣ J 9 5 2

South
♠ 10 5 2
♡ K 10 9 8 3
◇ Q 5
♣ K Q 10

The play was interesting and amusing. East won the first trick with the king of diamonds, then returned the ten of diamonds to South's queen. The declarer led the queen of clubs, West winning with the ace and switching to the *nine* of spades, suggesting no spade honour. Fooled by this good play, declarer panicked and called for dummy's ace of spades, then led a heart from the dummy. East rose with the ace, led a spade to his partner's king, received a spade ruff, and then led a diamond. This effected a trump promotion for the queen of hearts: three down and plus 800 to East–West.

I know that declarer misplayed by two(!) tricks as he should certainly finesse the queen of spades. But that's exactly what happens if you double a bad player. Finally, note that on a spade lead (probable without the double) declarer actually would have made his contract. Psychological doubles may be theoretically unsound but in practice they are very rewarding.

You can catch a good player too with these slightly speculative doubles – especially when he's partnered with a bad player. All you need to do is listen to the bidding. Take the following auction:

West	North	East	South
You	Bad Player	Partner	Good Player
		Pass	1 ♡
1 ♠	2 ♡	2 ♠	3 ♡[1]
3 ♠	4 ♡[2]	Pass	Pass
Dble[3]			

[1] When a good player bids three hearts, he has judged that his side cannot make game. (Three hearts by a good player in this sort of sequence is purely competitive. He would bid a new suit if he were interested in partner's co-operation in trying to bid a game.)
[2] The bad player makes the impossible and wrong bid for the thousandth time.
[3] Don't look at your hand – punish them. Trust the good player's judgment. If he didn't think he could make four hearts, then why should you?

Getting Doubled

Do you dread being doubled? 'Yes,' you say. Would it surprise you to learn that on occasions I love it? Actually sometimes I try very hard to get doubled. Yes, you heard me. After reading this, so will you.

Have you ever held a bad hand like:

♠ Q 10 9 5 4 2 ♡ 4 ◇ J 10 9 2 ♣ 9 2

You hear your partner open one notrump (12–14 points), and have your right-hand opponent double? At the time you bid two spades, happy to have a safe port in a storm. If you agree that the opponents probably have a game somewhere, next time you might decide to try a friendly psych in this position. Bid two clubs or even two hearts. The opponents will double, and then you run to two spades. Yes, it's probable they will now shrug off your little joke and bid their game. But sometimes – just sometimes – they will miscalculate and double you, which is what you were angling for. Put in another way: what can you lose?

However, remember two points: don't do this on every occasion – the opponents soon get wise. Make the psychic bid in a lower-ranking suit than the real one, just in case partner puts you back to your first suit; at least you can correct at the same level.

Bidding a short suit can often work too. You're West at favourable vulnerability, holding:

♠ 10 9 6 4 ♡ 8 5 3 ◇ K 9 8 4 3 ♣ 7

The bidding begins like this:

West	North	East	South
	1NT	2NT[1]	4 ♡
?			

[1] Unusual: a minor two-suiter.

What do you bid? Your thoughts should run along these lines: It's their hand. You *know* you would like to play in five diamonds (doubled). If you bid five diamonds directly, it's unlikely you'll be allowed to play there. A bid of five clubs will attract a double. Then a run-out to five diamonds might induce a rhythm double, your opponents thinking you are floundering.

Try this sometime; you'll be surprised how often it works.

I suppose I have Godzilla to thank for learning the following strategy.

I still remember the hand. It was during the late-night game at Stefan's. I had just cut the Apeman against two goodish players. Already smelling blood, they were like a pair of hungry Dobermans, straining at their leashes, ready to attack. Worse, I picked up this hand:

♠ – ♡ 5 4 2 ◇ Q J 10 7 6 ♣ 10 9 5 4 3

I'm not normally a coward, but cutting Godzilla, and holding this hand, is enough to scare anybody. Trouble loomed. Worse, he grunted out one spade. Already with visions of being dummy in five or six spades doubled with a 5–0 fit, I started thinking of ways to get out of my impending predicament.

These seemed to be my options:

1 I could double the opponents in a partscore – they might not redouble and the loss would be cheaper than the penalty about to hit us.
2 I could make an insufficient bid, then change it, barring Godzilla from further action. But that is unethical; and anyway these opponents were smart enough to waive the penalty just to let him keep bidding.
3 A bit drastic, I could resort to a violent solution. Suicide and murder were both possibilities – if slightly premature.

Eventually I decided just to pass and the bidding continued:

West	North	East	South
	Zia		Godzilla
			1 ♠
2 ♡	Pass	2 ♠[1]	?

[1] Usually a good high-card heart raise – a stronger bid than an immediate three or four hearts.

At this point, my partner started to think. The more he thought, the more I sweated. How many spades was he going to bid? When he finally made up his mind, his bid both surprised and delighted me. He said, 'Four diamonds.' Mentally, I apologized for doubting him. But now I had a new problem. If my right-hand opponent bid four hearts, I would have liked to raise to five diamonds, but these opponents would have realized that I would never raise Godzilla to the five-level unless I had a real mountain. No, that would have been a complete giveaway. They would surely have bid five hearts. I needed to find a way to buy the hand in five diamonds doubled. Any ideas? I bid four spades!

The prospect of Godzilla playing in four spades when he was looking at five trumps was too much for my left-hand opponent. He barked out a double. This was passed back to me, and I retreated immediately to five diamonds. Once more, a resounding double.

This was the full deal:

Dlr: South
Vul: Love All

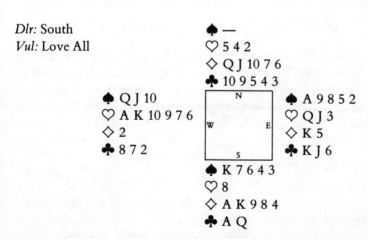

Not even the great ape could find a way to go down. I was full of praise, carefully not pointing out that he could have made an overtrick.

5

The Sting

Atlantic City, Monday Morning

Yesterday's nemesis, Mike the puzzle setter, appeared suddenly. 'Will you let me off the dinner I owe you if I give you some really good news?' He will do *anything* to avoid losing a bet! But for me it was at least a no-loss situation, so I agreed.

'You're going to be in the Pit for the qualifying rounds,' he informed me. Better – that really suited me. In some tournaments a 'pit' is set up to enable spectators to watch without disturbing the players or crowding on top of each other. This consists of a table set apart from the others around which chairs are placed in ascending rows, rather like a mini football stadium. In this way more people can watch in comfort for all – themselves and the players. I had been allocated the stationary position in the pit. Players would come to my table, play their three hands and leave. I would remain seated.

Why was it good news? For several reasons. Whereas some players become nervous at having too many spectators, others prefer it. Personally I love it. The showman in me somehow performs better when I am playing to a gallery. Second, the spectators will normally root for the stationary player, although their support is, of course, not vocal. Their well-wishes would be obvious and would make me the equivalent of the Home Team. Third, the fact that I wouldn't have to keep moving around, looking for the table, meant I would have more time to discuss my methods with my new partners – certainly a bonus.

The tournament lasted four days from Monday to Thursday. Everyone played for two days, after which the field was cut to 40 players for the two-day final. There was a consolation event for those who didn't make the final.

As the carryover of points from the qualifying stage (the first two days) was small, the tactics for those days were just to qualify; to play 'down the middle', avoiding disasters. Once in the final, it would be time to use the whip and be more aggressive.

The scoring was by international match points (imps), where the emphasis is on beating or making contracts and not taking risks by trying to make overtricks. It is like rubber bridge rather than pairs.

Once everyone was seated, the tournament director explained the movement and conditions of contest. There was pin-drop silence – the announcements were important and everyone listened intently. Each player reacts differently to this stage of a tournament. There are those, even experienced players, who feel tense and tight, sitting in silence until they feel the reassurance of the cards in their hands. Others can joke and talk, outwardly relaxed but inwardly readying themselves for the mental effort ahead. And it is an effort. The strain on a top expert's mind while he is in a tournament is incredible. I saw a survey that found that the level of concentration of a bridge expert is as intense as that of a brain surgeon in the operating theatre. The problems and vital points of bridge hands come up at any time, often when they are least expected. You need to be focused at all times; it is easy to miss the key moment, only to regret it bitterly a few seconds later.

It is possible to relax only when you are the dummy although even that can be difficult. There is one woman who has won several world championships who knits between hands, resting and recharging her batteries after bouts of intense concentration.

As the director finished giving his instructions, the familiar hum of conversation restarted. Boards of duplicated pre-dealt hands were being placed on the tables. Then a voice came over the public address system: 'Game time!'

The session started well and luckily for me. My first partner was Mike Passell, one of the very best American players. He is a professional 'hired gun' and ex-world champion. He is built like an American football player and plays as tough as he looks. Sitting South, he picked up this hand:

♠ A Q 6 4 3 ♡ 9 6 2 ◇ A Q 5 ♣ A Q

The bidding proceeded like this:

West	North	East	South
			1 ♠
Pass	2 ♠	Pass	3 ♡[1]
Pass	4 ♠	Pass	Pass
Pass			

[1] In principle, a game-try asking for help in hearts.

43

This was the full hand:

Dlr: South
Vul: East–West

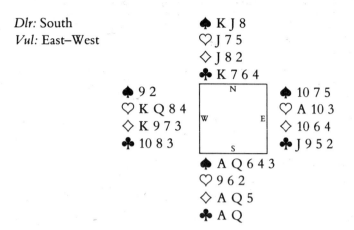

```
                    ♠ K J 8
                    ♡ J 7 5
                    ◇ J 8 2
                    ♣ K 7 6 4
  ♠ 9 2                              ♠ 10 7 5
  ♡ K Q 8 4          N               ♡ A 10 3
  ◇ K 9 7 3      W       E           ◇ 10 6 4
  ♣ 10 8 3                           ♣ J 9 5 2
                    S
                    ♠ A Q 6 4 3
                    ♡ 9 6 2
                    ◇ A Q 5
                    ♣ A Q
```

Once I responded two spades, Passell had every intention of going to game – but on the way there he stopped off to bid three hearts. He wanted to avoid a heart lead, which looked the most dangerous. So he took a little insurance: he bid the suit!

It worked when West decided to protect his heart holding and led a spade instead. Passell won in hand, unblocked the ace–queen of clubs, drew trumps ending in the dummy, and discarded a heart loser on the king of clubs. He lost one diamond and two heart tricks. Plus 420 was a great score.

That three-heart bid is the kind of action that costs nothing and often turns out to be very effective. Surprisingly, it is hardly used by anyone. You don't need to be a genius to make this strategy work for you. A heart lead defeats four spades, and that lead was made at most tables where the bidding went 1 ♠–2 ♠–4 ♠. I thanked Passell, who smiled in acknowledgment. It would have been bad manners to rub it in to our deflated opponents. Bad tactics too for the players now switched around and an opponent became my partner.

Let's take another look at that.

The words 'the sting' probably make you think of Paul Newman and Robert Redford, and 'the sting' is actually an expression used by the underworld to describe a 'con' – a kind of artistic thievery. Passell's phony game-try is a tactic among experts, the bridge equivalent of the sting. There are three common types of this deception: Sting Game-Tries, Sting Cue-Bids and Sting Splinters.

Sting Game-Tries

Try this hand from a recent money game. You are West, holding:

♠ J 5 4 ♡ Q 7 2 ◇ 10 9 6 2 ♣ A Q 10 9

The bidding proceeds:

West	North	East	South
			1 ♠
Pass	2 ♠	Pass	3 ♣
Pass	4 ♠	Pass	Pass
Pass			

What do you lead? Think about that for a moment.

Whenever you have a big hand and the auction starts like this:

West	North	East	South
You	LHO	Partner	RHO
1 ♡/♠	Pass	2 ♡/♠	Pass
?			

Partner has raised your opening. Before you bid on, *think*. If you have a hand with which you intend to bid game, but can see that a particular lead may be dangerous, consider trying to dissuade the opponents from leading that suit by bidding the suit on the way to game.

Sometimes you can even direct a favourable lead. Say you have a hand like this:

♠ J 10 9 5 4 ♡ A Q 4 ◇ A Q 7 ♣ A K

After partner raises one spade to two spades, you can see that a diamond or heart lead may well give you a trick. It costs little to bid three clubs to encourage the opponents to be a little friendly.

Now back to the lead problem. A trump looks right – you might have a lot of club winners if they aren't ruffed in the dummy. Sound thinking, but expensive: a clever South just 'stung' you. This was the full hand:

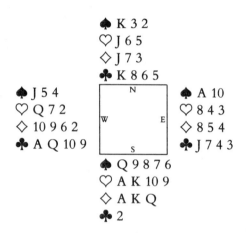

```
              ♠ K 3 2
              ♡ J 6 5
              ◇ J 7 3
              ♣ K 8 6 5
  ♠ J 5 4          N        ♠ A 10
  ♡ Q 7 2                   ♡ 8 4 3
  ◇ 10 9 6 2   W      E     ◇ 8 5 4
  ♣ A Q 10 9               ♣ J 7 4 3
                   S
              ♠ Q 9 8 7 6
              ♡ A K 10 9
              ◇ A K Q
              ♣ 2
```

South, always intending to bid four spades after his partner's raise, could see possible trump problems ahead. It would be nice if he could persuade West to lead a trump. But how?

By bidding his short suit, where West was likely to have strength and a desire to protect his tricks before they were ruffed away. Not too complicated, but very effective.

You don't need to be Garozzo to make such bids. The concept is simple enough for even the local palooka to soon master the theory. All you need is a little bit a larceny in your heart. However, I have a word of warning. If you use these ploys regularly at duplicate with your partner, you must inform the opponents about your style.

Bridge is a funny game. Stealing is encouraged, but holding back information is totally taboo.

Sting Cue-Bids

You've been losing all afternoon. Worse, the opponents have announced that this is to be that last rubber (they always seem to be in a rush when they're winning). You're steaming (trying to catch up), but at last you pick up an opening bid:

♠ A Q J 3 ♡ K 5 ◇ 8 7 4 ♣ A 6 5 3

The bidding starts like this:

West	North	East	South
	Partner		You
	1 ♡	Pass	1 ♠
Pass	3 ♠	Pass	?

At this point, a slam looks likely. What's more, your bank balance needs it. But what do *you* bid?

These are the apparent possibilities: four clubs (a cue-bid, hoping to hear four diamonds), four notrumps (checking up on aces), and six spades (a reasonable bash).

But I don't bid any of those! Think ahead.

You're scared of a diamond lead, but just in time you realize you're more scared of going home and admitting to your losses. You need to make a slam to avoid a row at home.

You try to stop the diamond lead and you *sting* with a four-diamond cue-bid. With a bit of luck and no diamond lead you might catch a dummy like this:

♠ K 10 8 4 ♡ A Q J 10 9 ◇ Q 2 ♣ K Q

The opponents may not fall for it next time, but that's next time – when you'll make the genuine cue-bid of four clubs!

Look out for the opportunity to make phony cue-bids: they come up all the time.

Sting Splinters

This one is for tournament players who are looking for a way to engineer a coup. Rubber-bridge players may not be able to use it.

A splinter bid (usually a double jump to show a fit for partner and shortness in the bid suit) is very useful. It is clear, concise and quick. It carries a lot of information, but it also helps the opponents as well as your partner. Suppose, as North, you hold:

♠ A J 10 4 ♡ A 7 6 ◇ 3 ♣ A K Q 10 6

The bidding starts like this:

West	North	East	South
	You		Partner
	1 ♣	Pass	1 ♠
Pass	?		

What do you bid?

A splinter bid of four diamonds is the 'normal' action, which may get you to a magic slam. However, it also pinpoints to your opponents the heart lead that may defeat four or six spades. Occasionally you might wish to consider the alternative of a 'phoney' splinter of three hearts (or four hearts). This will attract a diamond lead, which may well be vital.

Partner could have any one of these:

a ♠ K Q 7 6	b ♠ Q 9 5 3	c ♠ K 9 7 5 2
♡ K Q 3	♡ 9 5 4	♡ J 2
◇ 9 7 4	◇ K Q 6 5	◇ A 5 2
♣ 7 5 4	♣ J 8	♣ 8 7 2

With hand *a*, the phoney cue-bid will backfire. Looking at the supposed losers in diamonds, partner will sign off in four spades, whereas if you made the normal splinter of four diamonds, you might have reached the magic slam. Nothing works all the time!

However, with hand *b*, the four-diamond splinter attracts the feared heart lead. Now four spades goes one down if the trump finesse loses. After the four-heart splinter and a diamond lead, four spades make plus 450 or 480 (if the spade finesse wins).

Finally, with hand *c*, both splinters get you to the slam, but after a heart lead, your back is against the wall, hoping for some luck in one of the black suits. But after a diamond lead, you're practically lay down.

Save one of these bids for a rainy day when you want to live a little. It's a killer when it comes off. But people are getting so used to my coming up with this sort of craziness that if I make one of these bids, my opponents don't trust me. You, on the other hand, have probably got some time ahead before they wise up. So go ahead – *sting* a little.

London

I'm often asked how long it took me to learn to play well. That is a tough question. I suppose it was about two years before I felt I was ready to play against the best. But that was two years of playing almost daily, often for ten to twelve hours at a stretch.

Ten to twelve hours at a bridge table is unlike ten to twelve hours anywhere else. To say the time flies would be an understatement. 'Disappears' would be more accurate. At Stefan's, when Dr Manch, one of the most successful players at the club, was told how well I was doing in the lower-stake games, he always said, 'He's just lucky. Wait until he gets to my table. Then we'll show him how to play bridge.'

When I finally arrived at the big table, I learnt that winning can have its drawbacks. Stefan would calculate the total of the cheques of the players who 'knocked' (defaulted) after they lost to the expert. I must have been pretty hot because it wasn't long before Stefan gave me the dubious honour of stopping me playing – including at Manch's table – except on rare occasions.

'You're too good,' he would say. 'You'll ruin my business.'

The comment stroked my ego, but to be the best money player in a club was a long way from being a top international. It was time to try the tournament world.

Paradise

If you sat on your magic carpet in May and told it to take you to Paradise, it would head straight for the South of France. The sun shines, but not enough to burn; the beaches have bodies, but not unwelcome crowds – and that's only the aperitif.

The natural beauty of the country, the contrast between the blue of the Mediterranean and the splendour of the mountains, is superb, enough to enthrall even the most urban of tastes. Any visitor whose resistance is still not overcome by this would then be happily seduced by the best food on earth. Bouillabaisse, the fish soup, which is a speciality of the Côte d'Azur, is wonderful beyond description. And it is matched by the fabulous cooking of any of the restaurants that you just come across accidentally while exploring the region: La Chaumière, Villefranche, or Têtu in Antibes.

The French are brilliant – I say that because every year for a month or so in spring they hold a series of bridge tournaments on the Côte d'Azur. The locations include holiday resorts like Juan-les-Pins, Cannes and Monte Carlo. Unlike bridge tournaments in most countries (especially America) these are holidays first and bridge events second – with only one session of play a day. This is one reason why bridge is thriving in France. The games start at three or four in the afternoon and end at seven or eight – enough to whet your appetite but not enough to drown you.

Having decided to try the world of tournament bridge, my initial sortie was here, to the South of France. Teaming up with Martin Hoffman, a regular visitor to the continent, my first tournament was Juan-les-Pins. If you have to go to school, there's no harm going to one where they serve champagne with breakfast and where the discotheques never close.

The tournaments vary in length, and beginners and experts are both equally welcome and equally in evidence. The one in Juan lasts fourteen days. There are four events, the Individual, the Mixed Pairs, the Open Pairs and the Teams. You can enter as many or as few as you like.

We had arrived too late for the Individual. Let me tell you about the Mixed. For most players, a mixed pairs (with the exception of world championships) is a casual social outing. But there is still an art in doing well. Often the field is full of unbalanced partnerships with one better player (man or woman) playing under sufferance with his or her mate. It is a mutant form of the game where the senior partner tries to hog all the hands, and bids as if playing solo or cut-throat. But all the while they are trying to disguise what they are doing in order to retain their partner's dignity. It isn't easily done, which helps to explain why the Mixed can result in violent fights, tears, and shattered illusions – even broken marriages.

My idea of action during the two days of the Mixed was to browse lazily through a good book on the beach, with the occasional exercise of reaching out for a nearby cocktail. And that's exactly what I was doing when Hoffman came running up just half an hour before the start of the Mixed. He said, 'I've found you a partner for the Mixed.'

'What on earth are you talking about? You know I have no intention . . .'

My reply was interrupted by Martin. 'Here she is.'

I looked up. There are very few things that could have dragged me away from my idyllic resting-place and made me change my original plan. Monique just happened to be one of them. With sparkling green eyes and a soft, throaty voice, Monique was almost unreal. The closest I can get to describing her is to compare the feeling one gets from picking up a ten-card suit for the first time. A mixture of fantasy fulfilled and the surge of wild expectation. All in all, she was impossible to resist. Doubtless she couldn't play, but who would be watching her cards?

Bridge is a pure game, cerebral and intellectually satisfying. I think it is inappropriate, even disgusting, for one person to play with another simply because they find them physically attractive. But what could I do? I admit it – I am digusting. Anyway, Monique wasn't just attractive, she was a knockout.

Things didn't go well. In fact, the first day's game was a disaster. We were lying 180th out of a possible 190. It was caused by nervousness (Monique), bad luck and lust (me). Monique was close to tears at the end of play and rushed off. My dinner plans were ruined. I couldn't help thinking that this was no way to impress her.

Born out of the threat of frustrated romance, great ideas can sometimes emerge. So was born 'Le Pique Pakistani' (the Paki Spade): a system designed to bring the smile back to Monique's charming face and – hopefully – the love back to my life.

The theory was simple enough. Whenever either one of us was non-vulnerable and it was our turn to open the bidding, we would call one spade – regardless of strength or distribution. Partner could be scientific and respond one notrump with a good hand of thirteen-plus points as a kind of 'what have you got?' bid; or otherwise just play it by ear, trying to cause as much havoc as possible. After all, we couldn't do any worse!

We declared our system to our opponents, of course, and then *Jackpot!* The element of surprise, luck, fate, whatever – I don't really know – but good results poured in as the opponents succumbed to the devilishness of the system.

Here is an example:

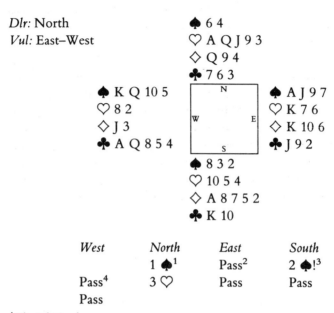

Dlr: North
Vul: East–West

North
♠ 6 4
♡ A Q J 9 3
♢ Q 9 4
♣ 7 6 3

West
♠ K Q 10 5
♡ 8 2
♢ J 3
♣ A Q 8 5 4

East
♠ A J 9 7
♡ K 7 6
♢ K 10 6
♣ J 9 2

South
♠ 8 3 2
♡ 10 5 4
♢ A 8 7 5 2
♣ K 10

West	North	East	South
	1 ♠[1]	Pass[2]	2 ♠![3]
Pass[4]	3 ♡	Pass	Pass
Pass			

[1] The Paki Spade.
[2] Stuck.
[3] Take that!
[4] S(t)ucker.

The opponents could have made four or five spades, rather luckily. But it was difficult for them to get to four spades when not only one but *both* opponents had bid spades. (Fifteen years later a similar but more refined method of destruction was devised in New Zealand, following its original invention in Poland. 'Fert' bids were inflicted on the bridge world – where opening bids of one diamond, one heart or one spade, depending upon vulnerability, would show 0–7 points. The 'fert' moniker is an abbreviation for fertilizer, used as the bids are intended to aid the growth of good results.) Le Pique Pakistani was before its time.

The upshot was that we moved up 140 places, finishing a respectable fortieth.

Monique was delighted.

I was delighted that Monique was delighted.

And the love affair?

I suppose you could say that we celebrated our success in the usual manner.

But if I thought the transition from rubber bridge to duplicate would be easy, I soon learnt otherwise. The rest of the tournament was undistinguished for me as far as results were concerned. But this just helped to bring home some of the fundamental differences between rubber and tournament bridge.

Rubber bridge is a jungle where survival comes first. You are on your own, and the emphasis is on improvisation and adaptability. In the final analysis, the key to success is doing the right thing to suit the conditions. Your individual instinct and ability are your weapons. The tournament world, in contrast, is closer to an arena, where well-trained and well-armed gladiators fight. The key is to succeed through better preparation, and by functioning as an efficient unit with your partner. They are different games, and both offer their own types of equally pleasurable satisfaction. I would say that rubber is more 'human' and the tournament game more 'pure', closer to par, and where methods take the place of judgment and guesswork.

To give you just one example, in the tournament North opened one notrump (strong). The next player, East, had this hand:

♠ K 3 ♡ A Q 10 4 ◇ 6 ♣ K Q 10 9 8 3.

In a rubber-bridge game, you would overcall two clubs and play there. But in duplicate the two-club overcall is rarely used in this unnatural way.

West's hand was:

♠ 7 6 4 2 ♡ K 9 8 3 ◇ 8 7 5 2 ♣ A.

Tournament players have methods to deal with hands like this. East bid a conventional two clubs, showing hearts and another suit. Now four hearts was easy to reach, West jumping to three hearts and East going on to game. As you can see, having an understanding or method to deal with a particular situation can be more useful than any amount of skill.

After Juan we drove down the coast to Cannes. Cannes: Movie stars, the Carlton Hotel, lobsters, Goulash (a form of bridge popular in France in which the cards aren't shuffled, leading to voids and nine-card suits becoming everyday occurrences), and a tournament shorter in duration than Juan's. We did slightly better, finishing in the money. I liked the tournament, and have returned regularly over the years. The best result I ever had there was in 1988 while playing with the brilliant young Indian player Jaggy Shivdasani – though it was almost a disaster. But before describing that incident, what was I, a Pakistani, doing playing with an

Indian, the traditional enemy?

I don't know – put it down to just another instance of the way in which bridge doesn't seem to allow people to know or care where they come from. It is impervious to society's traditional barriers of age, colour, religion or beliefs. Put it down to the magic, the spell that the game mysteriously weaves, bewitching all those who come into contact with it.

This was Jaggy's first trip to the South of France. A very talented player, whose enthusiasm at the table is a reflection of his attitude to life, he is the text-book tourist, always ready with his camera to go on any excursion. He bubbles excitedly through life.

We had an enormous session of 70 per cent on the first day of the Open Pairs. This is the equivalent of scoring a hat-trick of goals; and we were leading the field. It was about one in the afternoon on the final day's play. I was where I belonged, blissfully asleep, when the phone rang.

'*Help*,' a voice screamed.

'Excuse me,' I muttered, still drowsy. I wasn't reacting too well.

'Help me, I'm stuck.'

At last I recognized Jaggy's voice. He went on to explain that he had gone on a boat excursion to an island off the coast. Busy clicking away, engrossed in using up rolls of film, he had misunderstood the departure time of the boat and when he got back to the departure point, he was in time to see the boat sailing away. The next boat wasn't due until three, which was also the time the game was due to start. This meant he would be at least half an hour late.

Jaggy was on the verge of winning his first international tournament and fate had stranded him on an island five miles away. He was desperate, and he pleaded with me to hire a boat to save him.

'Do something, wake up, get up, go to the dock and pay a fisherman to sail out and rescue me,' he pleaded. 'But look for one with an old boat. That might be cheaper,' he added as an afterthought.

Where was I going to find a sympathetic French fisherman prepared to rescue a bridge playing Indian savage who was marooned on a not so desert island? Just trying to explain the predicament in my limited French was likely to get me locked up. And it's a fact that most Frenchmen refuse to speak English even if they can understand it. I seriously contemplated going back to sleep. I was probably dreaming anyway.

On the other hand, as far as I knew, this was the first time that a Pakistani and an Indian had ever teamed up in international competition – it would be a great bonus if we won. I tried this line on the concierge, but sadly this appeal to a higher ideal was totally wasted on him. He did react sympathetically to a 200-franc note and promised to make enquiries, which, naturally, proved to be fruitless.

As a last resort, I appealed to the highest authority – the Tournament Director. I was ready with my pathetic story of the dangers of travelling in a foreign land. He was surprisingly understanding and agreed sportingly to give us a maximum of half an hour's grace during which I could play with a substitute. I told Jaggy this when he called back, adding a few choice descriptions of my views about his lineage, using some of the words that are common to both Urdu (the Pakistani language) and Hindi (the Indian language).

The story had a happy ending. Jaggy managed to make it before the deadline, and though physically slightly the worse for wear, his bridge skills were not dimmed. I remember a great hand he played, but first some instruction, some advice that may seem out of the Twilight Zone. In defence, every time you have a nine, think about playing it at the first opportunity.

You read me; stay with me, I'm not crazy!

Most people know that they should (although they never do) play the nine in these positions:

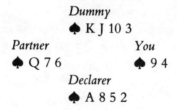

Dummy
♠ K J 10 3

Partner   *You*
♠ Q 7 6   ♠ 9 4

Declarer
♠ A 8 5 2

Declarer cashes the ace: *drop the nine*.

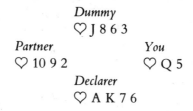

Dummy

♡ J 8 6 3

Partner   *You*

♡ 10 9 2   ♡ Q 5

Declarer

♡ A K 7 6

When declarer cashes the ace, *play the nine.* Declarer may now cross to dummy and call for the jack, which caters both for a 4–1 break and which wins if you started with the ten–nine doubleton. Or he may lead low from his hand on the second round.

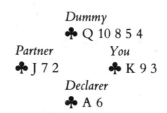

Dummy

◇ K Q 10 5

You   *Partner*

◇ J 9 6 4   ◇ 3

Declarer

◇ A 8 7 2

When declarer leads low towards the dummy, put in the nine. Declarer will probably cash the queen next, playing your partner for ◇ J 6 4 3.

Dummy

♣ Q 10 8 5 4

Partner   *You*

♣ J 7 2   ♣ K 9 3

Declarer

♣ A 6

Play the nine under the ace. Declarer's 'correct' play now is low to the queen.

 In all these situations, playing the nine cannot cost, and may win a trick. If nothing else, it keeps declarer under pressure.

How about this one?

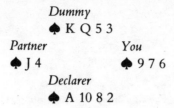

Dummy
♠ K Q 5 3

Partner   You
♠ J 4   ♠ 9 7 6

Declarer
♠ A 10 8 2

Left to his own devices, declarer will always start with the king, then the queen. However, if you play the nine under the king, he will now cross to the ace at the second trick, allowing for your having a singleton. This may be useful if you want him to use up a hand entry prematurely. Playing the nine can transfer the tempo of playing a suit from the declarer to the defenders.

Here's an example:

Dlr: South
Vul: Game All

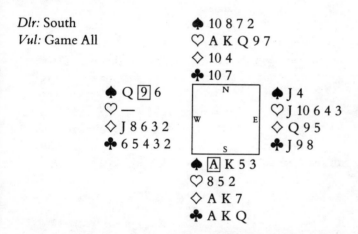

♠ 10 8 7 2
♡ A K Q 9 7
♢ 10 4
♣ 10 7

♠ Q 9 6
♡ —
♢ J 8 6 3 2
♣ 6 5 4 3 2

♠ J 4
♡ J 10 6 4 3
♢ Q 9 5
♣ J 9 8

♠ A K 5 3
♡ 8 5 2
♢ A K 7
♣ A K Q

South arrived in six spades, and West led the six of clubs. Declarer won in hand and cashed the ace of spades. If West had followed with the six, declarer would have had no option but to play for trumps to break 3–2. However, when West followed with the nine, declarer played 'safe' by leading a low trump out of his hand in case East started with four spades. In this case that led to disaster. East won with the jack of spades and gave his partner a heart ruff.

The nine can work overtime – not many are aware of the following positions in notrump contracts.

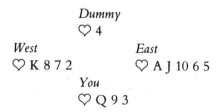

Dummy
♡ 4

West   East
♡ K 8 7 2   ♡ A J 10 6 5

You
♡ Q 9 3

Your left-hand opponent leads the two; because you have the nine, you can block the suit. If East wins with the ace and returns the jack, you cover with the queen. West has to win the fourth round of the suit. Alternatively if East returns the five or six, the nine prevents the defence from taking their obvious five tricks.

Dummy
♢ Q 9 2

West   East
♢ K 10 8 7   ♢ A J 6 5 4

You
♢ 3

West leads the seven: you insert the nine to hold them to four immediate tricks. So, treat the nine with respect; use it to terrify and mislead declarers. Start throwing it around even if you're not always sure why.

Jaggy must share my views; watch him in action.

Dlr: South
Vul: North–South

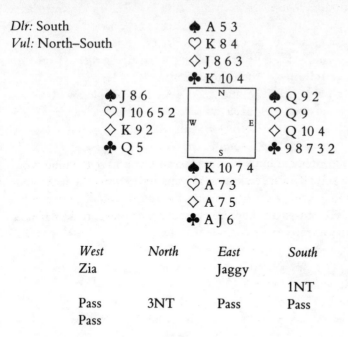

♠ A 5 3
♡ K 8 4
◇ J 8 6 3
♣ K 10 4

♠ J 8 6
♡ J 10 6 5 2
◇ K 9 2
♣ Q 5

♠ Q 9 2
♡ Q 9
◇ Q 10 4
♣ 9 8 7 3 2

♠ K 10 7 4
♡ A 7 3
◇ A 7 5
♣ A J 6

West	North	East	South
Zia		Jaggy	
			1NT
Pass	3NT	Pass	Pass
Pass			

I led the five of hearts to Jaggy's queen. South won the second round with the ace, then cashed the king of spades. Jaggy played the nine!

South could no longer afford to duck my eight on the next round, putting up the ace. Jaggy unblocked the queen.

Now I could win the third round of spades and clear the hearts.

South had eight tricks, and knowing that East had eight minor-suit cards to my five, misguessed the queen of clubs. One down, and a big step forwards in Pakistan–India relationships.

Winning has its own satisfaction, and although no one except me seemed particularly impressed with the political magnitude of our achievement, I was sufficiently moved to write off the 200FF.

After Cannes comes Monte Carlo. The mention of Monte Carlo con-jures up images of the jet set: of extravagance, elegance and beauty. For once, reality fits the image. The only thing small about Monte Carlo is its size – a mere two square kilometres, or about half the size of Central Park in New York.

The marriage of the beautiful Grace Kelly to her handsome prince gave the municipality a fairy-tale aura. The fascination of the world with royalty and glamour has done the rest. Wealth is still the key word, but banking, not gambling, is the principal industry. The rich move there not only to enjoy the playground but also for the more commercial reason that residents don't pay any taxes. Prices are astronomical, so be careful where you order a drink. The first time I was there, I offered someone a coke at Jimmy's, the famous night club, and it cost me £20.

However, no mention of Monte Carlo would be complete without an Omar story. Breaking the bank at Monte Carlo is every gambler's dream, but it's much more likely the bank will break you. That doesn't always have to be as bad as it sounds – if you are a superstar like Omar Sharif. Omar once found himself at the losing end of a heavy night at the chemin de fer table. In fact, in bridge terminology, heavy was an under-bid: he had lost everything he had, a small fortune.

Unfortunately, movie stars are not supposed to react to these setbacks like the other mortals. So he started to leave the casino with as much dignity as his acting skills would permit. He had almost made it to the exit when a man stopped him. 'Excuse me, Mr Sharif, I am sorry about your loss.' He spoke in Arabic.

'Thank you, but it was nothing. These things happen.'

'I am a great fan of yours, and hope you will accept a tip from me that might help you recoup your losses. The price of silver is about to rise dramatically; buy some.'

Omar took the advice, and the next day called a friend of his, Alan 'Ace' Greenberg, President of Bear Sterns (an investment bank in New York), and also a keen bridge player. The tip was dynamite; a coup was in progress in the silver market and Omar not only recovered his losses, but made a profit as well.

I visited Monte Carlo many times over the next few years, but sadly the annual tournament there has been discontinued, probably from a lack of sponsorship. The last time I was there, I was a spectator, not a player, in the 1976 World Championships. Every fourth year each country may send teams to compete in the Open and Women's Team events.

There are no money prizes, of course, but the competition is as fierce as it is in any other bridge event. A world championship gold medal is the most treasured prize for any duplicate player. Many teams featured players I knew well. I was jealous that they could represent their countries at this level. I too would have liked to be playing for Pakistan, but that seemed no more than a hopeless dream.

6

Bridge is More Than Just
Holding Hands

Atlantic City, Monday Evening

During the first day's play, my emotions kept racing from the heights to the depths, keeping pace with the results I achieved. But coming towards the end of the session, I felt reasonably satisfied with the day's play. Most of my partners had played well, and we had kept the number of errors to an acceptable minimum. I expected my score to be reasonable – it is an odd aspect of bridge that, unlike any other game or sport, you don't know your score until the end of the session. You have an approximate idea, but it isn't confirmed until some fifteen minutes after play finishes, when the scores are posted.

Getting up from the table, I bumped into two old friends who were screaming at each other, and who looked on the verge of warfare. One of them, 'Harry the Horse', was almost breathing fire as he snapped, snorted and screamed at his companion, Fred. Both are from New York and play regularly in the big money games there; but that is all they have in common. Harry, straight out of *Guys and Dolls*, is about 6'6" and makes a living the hard way: betting on the horses. He is said to win over a million dollars a year doing this, but Harry never admits to anything where money is concerned. He certainly doesn't look a million dollars: if you passed him in the street you'd be more likely to offer him a dollar for a cup of soup than to ask him for a loan. As far as I can make out, Harry seems to possess only one shirt – I'd tell you the colour but it is no longer possible to define it with any degree of exactness; and his favourite pair of checked trousers have long lost any pretence at fashion. Harry has his good points and his bad points. It is true that on occasion he doesn't smell too sweet, but to be fair he could tell you the finishing times and prices of all the Kentucky Derby winners for the past ten years without even breathing hard. When he's not betting, Harry plays bridge. Harry loves bridge. He reads all the books, learns all the plays, knows all the conventions. Harry is a competent player, but he has one problem: he can't win; he doesn't even finish. Harry has won six-figure sums at the racetrack in an afternoon; in a bridge tournament he has been placed several times, but nobody ever remembers him finishing in the winners' circle. There, he's on a permanent losing streak.

Fred on the other hand is a Taiwanese who settled in America. An engineer by trade, he came to this country as a student, got caught up in the American dream and stayed. He works for a construction company by day and moonlights at bridge by night to support his ever growing family. Fred is charming and well liked by everyone, but he becomes a cold and tough competitor when he sits at the bridge table. He wins consistently at money bridge but, like a lot of money players, is normally not too interested in tournaments and trophies. This tournament was the exception because of the high rewards. Without being technically much better than Harry, Fred does the right thing when it's needed – the mark of a winner.

Bridge quarrels and 'fights' are inevitable. It doesn't make any difference how much you play. It is always easy for the result on a particular hand to drive one or both players over the edge. Rather like a duel, the argument continues until one party gets satisfaction – which usually entails his partner (the perpetrator) apologizing to him, or a third party being brought in to adjudicate and apportion blame. It looked like I was to be the third party in this particular fight. The Horse was getting nowhere, so he grabbed hold of me. Foaming at the mouth, he announced, 'One of us needs a doctor, and it isn't me. Just tell this uneducated idiot that he doesn't understand the first thing about bidding, will you. You have this hand:

$$\spadesuit\ 9\ 4\quad \heartsuit\ A\ J\ 10\ 7\ 6\ 3\quad \diamondsuit\ A\ Q\ 5\quad \clubsuit\ 6\ 2$$

'The bidding began like this:

West	North	East	South
	Fred		Harry
	2 ♣[1]	Pass	2 ♡
4 ♢[2]	6 ♣	Pass	?

[1] Strong, artificial and forcing.
[2] Pre-emptive, natural.

'What would you have bid?'

This was tough. On the one hand, it looked as if I had a lot of tricks for

62

partner; on the other hand, the unwritten law in these situations where one partner jumps to slam, is that you should 'leave him alone' unless you are absolutely certain he can make seven. It was a close decision worthy of thought, but I was more interested in seeing the results of the afternoon's game than standing here any longer. I decided that Fred is a big boy, that the diamond holding looked dangerous, probably being opposite a void, and that if all my partner had needed was two aces, he could have used Blackwood. I said, 'I pass.'

Fred was beaming but Harry became more furious than before. He shouted, 'You are useless, just as bad as he is. I bid the obvious seven clubs, and they doubled. Of course I converted to seven notrumps in case they were ruffing something, and they doubled again. Then they cashed an ace. Would you believe it?'

C'est la vie, I thought. This was the layout:

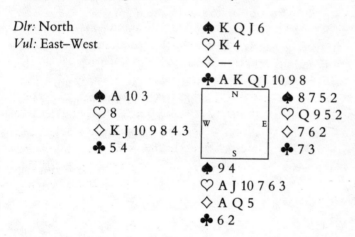

Dlr: North
Vul: East–West

North: ♠ K Q J 6 ♡ K 4 ◇ — ♣ A K Q J 10 9 8

West: ♠ A 10 3 ♡ 8 ◇ K J 10 9 8 4 3 ♣ 5 4

East: ♠ 8 7 5 2 ♡ Q 9 5 2 ◇ 7 6 2 ♣ 7 3

South: ♠ 9 4 ♡ A J 10 7 6 3 ◇ A Q 5 ♣ 6 2

At the time I sympathized slighty with Harry, but later, on looking deeper, I changed my mind, feeling that seven clubs was an inferior bid. This is why:

1 Two hearts had already shown a positive with hearts.
2 We had been pre-empted – a signal for caution.
3 South had two aces; if that was all partner wanted, he would have asked for them via Blackwood.
4 Partner took control of the auction. To overrule him required certainty, not conjecture.

Anyway, by now Harry had had his fill of both me and Fred. He stormed off, none too pleased.

Finally I was free to look at the results board. I expected to be well placed, but found that I wasn't even in the first twenty – I was lying twenty-third. Good enough to qualify, but not as comfortably placed as I would have liked, or had thought I would be. I had been feeling pretty high, as is customary when you think you have done well, but now my mood changed totally. I was annoyed and frustrated. Then I remembered that I had a dinner appointment. I just had time for a shower and change before we were due to meet.

I was still feeling disappointed. Expectation is a double-edged and powerful emotion. In bridge it can be treacherous. On occasions it lifts you to great heights, only a moment later to flick you down again. If I had played badly and been out of luck, I would have felt relieved and happy at a standing of twenty-third, with forty to qualify. But having expected to be among the leaders, I was shattered by my disappointing position. The feeling is so similar to the emotional ups and downs of being in love. Both give you high expectations that can lead both to despair and ecstasy. The pleasure of success is increased by comparison with the agony of failure. This is one of the reasons why bridge is so endlessly fascinating. No matter how much you play, or how proficient you become, you can never be in total control. While climbing out of the shower, I was appeased slightly by my own philosophizing. I accepted that there was nothing I could do about it; I would just have to play better tomorrow.

At least I had more chance than players in Pakistan had started with.

Pakistan, 1977

It wasn't bridge but politics that was responsible for my next move. Our business was going well, and my brother's thoughts once more reverted to politics. The government had changed in Pakistan, with the opposition party gaining power and he became a senator. Family is family, so I returned home for a while to run the business while he concentrated on his political affairs. (However, I did commute to London regularly for rubber-bridge fixes.)

Throughout my years spent abroad, I had always looked forward to regular visits back home. Even though the number of days spent there have been few by comparison, I have always identified closely with my country of birth, and have always thought of it as 'home'.

I may have been educated in the West, grown up with Western culture, and lived in countries of the West, but I feel that I am no more than a visitor. I love London, enjoy Paris, and find the excitement of New York thrilling, but it doesn't matter how long I've been away, whenever I head back to Pakistan, I feel the reassuring comfort and security that only going home can bring.

I'm not sure why my loyalties are so strong. Perhaps it's connected to the nostalgia of seeing the house I knew as a child, the warmth at greeting family and friends. It might be no more than sentimentality, but maybe it's more, something deeper, an inseparable bond with a culture to which I belong – but hardly know.

Sometimes it's hard to envisage how different the world can be; how cultures and customs vary from place to place as dramatically as the weather or the seasons. And how what is 'normal' in one part of the world is an anathema in another.

Even if you are one of those who occasionally reflects on such things, you would never think that such differences could apply to the game of bridge – but they do. Bridge is a harmless pastime in most countries, but there are some nations left where even today the word 'bridge' is viewed suspiciously by the powers that be. There, either because of a lack of education or understanding of the game, it is viewed as an activity more closely related to gambling than to an intellectual contest. I should know, because Pakistan is one of those countries.

Ever since watching the 1976 World Championships in Monte Carlo, I had thought about the possibility of Pakistan's participating internationally. *Even though I was theoretically eligible, it never occurred to me to consider representing any other country.* The problem was that I knew my hopes were unlikely to materialize because of the 'anti' attitudes in my homeland. How do you represent a country in a sport that isn't a sport?

Until 1977 there wasn't even an official bridge club. Then one, just one, opened. It might not occur to you, as you visit your local bridge club, that you are doing something exciting, let alone dangerous. After all, what could be more mundane than a relaxed afternoon at the local club? 'Mundane' would not be accurate to describe the atmosphere in our bridge club. In 1975, a bridge club was opened by a group of enthusiasts who wanted to hold a weekly duplicate game. The club lasted just one week! That's how long it took for the religious groups of the area to find out about it and have it closed.

In a way it was just as well; simply visiting the club was nerve-racking with the constant worry that at any time violent neighbours might turn up with their own brand of eviction notice.

We were ready to jump off the nearest balcony at the first sign of danger. The term 'skip bid' took on a new dimension . . .

After this mild attempt at organization, we slunk back to the privacy of our own houses for a while. But bridge players all over the world are a resilient lot, ours being more tenacious than most. Undaunted, they formed a Bridge Association, and even applied to the Government for recognition. This recognition was not immediately forthcoming, but meanwhile a compromise was reached. The good news was that we would be allowed to open a bridge club. The bad news was that it would have to be located in the changing room of the National Sports Stadium. The room was off the beaten track, dingy and tiny. But it was a start. Then a lucky break occurred. The Pakistan Bridge Association received an invitation to send a team to participate in the Far East Championships in Hong Kong.

Once more we faced government opposition, this time for reasons of international politics because capitalist Taiwan was being represented. We would not be allowed to play against them, because of the objection from Mainland China. Another compromise; we had to give them a walkover whenever we were scheduled to play against them. Naturally that meant we had almost no chance of doing really well; but then again these were trying times. At least we were allowed to enter the competition: before you can win you must enter the race.

Forming a team, the next step, was easy. We simply invited anyone to show up who was prepared to pay his own expenses. We just managed to get six players. Reinforced with a few officials along for the ride, the Pakistan National Bridge Team had entered the world arena.

Not surprisingly, the opposition weren't particularly impressed by this team of newcomers, and for the most part disposed of us rather efficiently. The only bright spot was that in our first outing we did beat India, allowing us to save a little face on our return home. The rivalry between Pakistan and India is such that beating them is as important for us as winning a World Championship is for anyone else.

These excursions into the Far East became an annual event, and although not even the most generous would say that bridge in Pakistan was exactly booming, it was at least a start. It had the effect of stirring the martini of interest, if not shaking it too violently. Each year a few more people became available for selection. How much this was due to the love of bridge and how much to the attraction of visiting one of the many exotic oriental countries, I'm not sure.

Most of our players are very emotional, but we quickly learnt that team spirit and behaviour were almost as important as how well we played. We devised our own set of rules. Apologizing for an error can be very difficult, so we even incorporated an 'I'm sorry partner' bid in our system:

West	North	East	South
	1NT	Pass	2 ♠[1]
Pass	2NT	Pass	3 ♠[2]

[1] A transfer to two notrumps.
[2] A transfer to 3NT with the message 'Sorry about that previous hand, partner.'

Three spades had no other meaning in our methods. The opener had no idea what the responder held, but it worked and never failed to raise a smile.

Our next task was to form partnerships and a regular team. This was harder than it sounds because our few good players were spread all over the world. I was lucky to find a partner, Masood Salim, whose composure was well suited to my more exuberant style. At that time his English was limited. He had never read a bridge book, but his natural talent was enormous. We are still going strong some fifteen years later.

Masood is one of the few partners with whom I feel confident when laying down my dummy. In one of our excursions, he showed his flair on the following deal when he made a four-spade contract by completely fooling the player in the West position. He did this by making a rare double-duck, which demonstrates the importance of imagination in bridge.

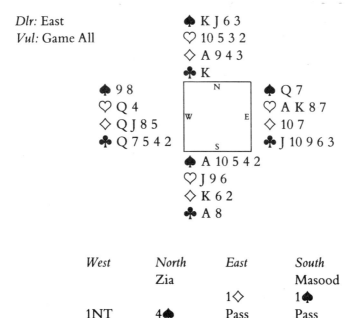

Dlr: East
Vul: Game All

♠ K J 6 3
♡ 10 5 3 2
◇ A 9 4 3
♣ K

♠ 9 8
♡ Q 4
◇ Q J 8 5
♣ Q 7 5 4 2

♠ Q 7
♡ A K 8 7
◇ 10 7
♣ J 10 9 6 3

♠ A 10 5 4 2
♡ J 9 6
◇ K 6 2
♣ A 8

West	North	East	South
	Zia		Masood
		1◇	1♠
1NT	4♠	Pass	Pass
Pass			

The bidding requires some explanation. The New Zealand pair sitting East–West were playing a high-tech system of relays and computer-like sequences. East's opening bid of one diamond was artificial. It meant he had 10–15 points and no five-card major. He couldn't open one club because, in this system, that would have been strong, showing sixteen-plus points.

Then, after Masood, South, made the normal one-spade overcall, West bid an 'unusual' one notrump, which meant he had the minors. Sitting North, I decided to end all this nonsense by leaping to game.

West led the queen of diamonds, and Masood studied the hand before playing to the opening lead, a practice that average players would do well to copy. With four obvious red-suit losers, Massood's only chance seemed to be pitch one of his hearts on dummy's fourth diamond. But this would require losing a diamond trick, thus giving the opponents the chance to cash their three heart tricks.

Rather than expose the situation, Masood ducked in both hands, pretending that he didn't hold the king of diamonds.

Pity poor West, who had to find a heart shift to defeat the contract. Instead, he continued diamonds at trick two noting the fall of East's ten. Masood thanked him silently, winning with the King, then drew two rounds of trumps. He now led a diamond from his hand, finessing dummy's nine. On the ace of diamonds, Masood discarded a losing heart.

This beautiful double-duck not only succeeded in fulfilling the contract, but it also put a psychological damper on our opponents' outlook for the rest of the match. Players do not like it when an opponent makes a game that could have been defeated. They like it even less when they are fooled in the process – which is one reason I enjoy playing with Masood: if I am his partner, he can never do it to me!

The pot of gold waiting for the winner of the Zonal Tournament was the opportunity to play in the World Championship for the Bermuda Bowl, easily the most coveted prize in bridge. Every two years the winners of the various zonal tournaments around the world would meet at the play-offs – something like the Davis Cup in tennis.

Such lofty ambitions were still not in our sights, although our standings did improve with experience. If only we weren't restricted by our walkover loss to Taiwan – but that would take a miracle.

Meanwhile, friendly competition with India *was* on the menu. If you leave behind the rhetoric of the politicians, the people of India and Pakistan are really very close. We are two countries but one people. Thousands of families have members in both countries, and memories of days gone by are still very much alive, especially in the hearts of the older generation. Each year we would look forward to attending the December Bridge Congress in Calcutta.

Calcutta is without a doubt amongst the dirtiest and dustiest cities in the world. The population is so huge that, at almost any time of the day or night, the crowds on the pavements outnumber in density a combined concert of Madonna and the Rolling Stones. Yet, Calcutta is also the most special city in the world – for its people. A voyager could travel the world without encountering anything comparable to Calcutta's overwhelming warmth and hospitality. And this is in a country already famous for its kindness to visitors. Tourists traverse the world to see its various wonders. This is Calcutta's wonder, and in itself sufficient reason to visit the city.

The actual play was held at the Saturday Club, where the picturesque green lawns still echo with the ghosts of the British Raj. There were literally hundreds of kibitzers (spectators) crowding around our table at the start of the play in the pairs. The sheer numbers of these enthusiasts forced the organizers to move our table from the playing hall into the spacious gardens behind. Although this slightly inconvenienced the East–West pairs who had to make the detour, it was in practice the only way to accommodate the throng.

I remember this hand:

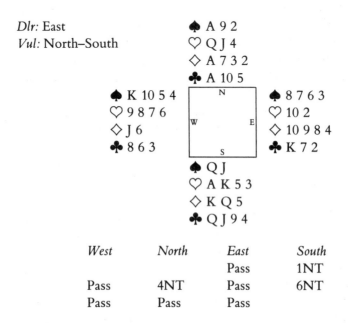

Dlr: East
Vul: North–South

♠ A 9 2
♡ Q J 4
◇ A 7 3 2
♣ A 10 5

♠ K 10 5 4
♡ 9 8 7 6
◇ J 6
♣ 8 6 3

♠ 8 7 6 3
♡ 10 2
◇ 10 9 8 4
♣ K 7 2

♠ Q J
♡ A K 5 3
◇ K Q 5
♣ Q J 9 4

West	North	East	South
		Pass	1NT
Pass	4NT	Pass	6NT
Pass	Pass	Pass	

Officially the one-notrump opening by Debashis Roy showed 15–17 points, but he not unreasonably devalued the queen-jack doubleton of spades and counted his 18 points as 17.

The opening lead was the nine of hearts. Assuming the king of clubs was badly placed, South saw that he needed a diamond break, or a winning spade finesse, or a squeeze (if one defender held the king of spades and four diamonds). But if the diamonds were not breaking, should he play for the spade finesse or the squeeze?

Roy had an ace up his sleeve (or should I say a jack). He determined to use the fact that he was a point heavy for his opening bid. Roy won the opening heart lead in hand and finessed the queen of clubs, losing to the king. He won the heart return in the dummy, cashed the jack of hearts and ace of clubs, then returned to hand with the queen of diamonds. He played off his fourth heart and the jack of clubs.

At this point, West had seen fifteen points in declarer's hand. So, when Roy led the queen of spades, can you blame West for covering, 'knowing' that South couldn't have the jack? Roy was able to claim.

If the queen of spades hadn't been covered, Roy would have taken the inference that West didn't have the king. He would have put up dummy's ace of spades and played for a squeeze against East. Neat!

Two incidents stand out.

While playing in Calcutta I met an unforgettable bridge player, a young man called Om Parkash Chaudry. Memorable, not for his standard of play, which was high enough, but because he was blind. More, he played without the benefit of Braille cards. A friend would sit behind him, whispering to him just once what his cards were as he picked them up. Similarly, if Om became the declarer, his friend would name dummy's cards as well. Om would call his cards whenever it was his turn to play either on defence or as declarer. He rarely made a mistake, and would do this hand after hand, playing not only well but at normal speed.

The first time I saw him, I was impressed and asked him to play in a tournament with me. He agreed, and we played a few days later in a pairs event. We were doing well enough and Om was in the middle of playing a hand, when the electricity failed, a not uncommon occurrence in India.

The play around him stopped, but Om, oblivious to what was happening, continued calling for a card from the dummy.

'You'll have to wait, the lights have gone out,' I informed him. Before I realized the significance of my own remark, Om answered, 'I'm sorry, I forgot that you can't play bridge with the lights out.' Just an innocent statement, but a lesson at the same time, equally valuable in life and bridge. Try to understand a situation from the other person's point of view. Things often look very different from the other side.

The second incident was more humorous. When I had started to play bridge seriously, I remember people asking me, 'Just how far can bridge take you?' It was in Calcutta that I might have found the answer to that question. It started with an opening lead problem, one that literally took our team from Calcutta to Delhi.

You hold:

♠ 8 3 ♡ 8 7 5 ♢ K 7 6 3 ♣ K 8 7 5

The bidding goes as follows:

West	North	East	South
	1 ♣[1]	Pass	2 ♣[2]
Pass	2 ♡	Pass	2 ♠
Pass	3 ♠	Pass	4 ♣
Pass	4 ♡	Pass	4 ♠
Pass	4NT[3]	Pass	5 ♢[4]
Pass	6 ♠	Pass	Pass
Pass			

[1] Precision: at least sixteen points.
[2] Eight-plus points and at least five clubs.
[3] Roman Key Card Blackwood.
[4] One key card, counting the four aces and the king of spades as key cards.

What would you lead?

At the time I had a penchant for leading honours whenever possible, probably because I thought it looked good. It is not usual practice, so a player who succeeds in this play stands out. But here it also happened to be technically correct. The king of diamonds *was* the only lead to defeat the contract. The full deal looked like this:

Dlr: North
Vul: Game All

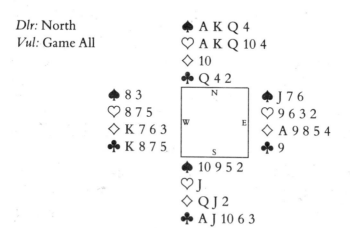

♠ A K Q 4
♡ A K Q 10 4
♢ 10
♣ Q 4 2

♠ 8 3
♡ 8 7 5
♢ K 7 6 3
♣ K 8 7 5

♠ J 7 6
♡ 9 6 3 2
♢ A 9 8 5 4
♣ 9

♠ 10 9 5 2
♡ J
♢ Q J 2
♣ A J 10 6 3

On a low diamond lead, declarer is able to take a ruffing finesse on the second round to establish a discard for dummy's club loser.

The good thing about such plays is that if they fail, they are hidden away, whereas if they work, they get great press. This was the case here, but the story didn't end there.

A few days later our team had to fly to Delhi. We arrived at Calcutta Airport to find that a bureaucratic slip-up had resulted in our not having the required visas. Travel through India is restricted for Pakistanis, and so we were told that we would have to wait two or three days. A situation that could have turned out to be rather annoying was saved by my lead in Calcutta. When we discovered one of the senior officials was a bridge fanatic who had been following the results at the tournament, we appealed to him. Ignoring the usual red tape, he granted permission on condition I answered just one question: 'How on earth did you lead the king of diamonds?'

This is what I explained: 'The way to tackle a lead problem is to analyse the bidding. What do we know? North has at least five hearts and four spades, while South has four spades and at least five clubs. There must be a key card missing, otherwise North would have tried for seven. North has no more than four minor-suit cards. His use of Blackwood means that he has a diamond control, my king of diamonds confirming that it is the ace or a singleton. It must be right to attack diamonds before any losers in that suit can be pitched on good hearts.

'Can it make any difference which diamond to lead? Yes. If North has a singleton and South has a dangerous holding like ◇ A J 10 or ◇ Q J 4, leading a low diamond to partner's queen or ace would allow declarer to make an extra trick later by taking a ruffing finesse. If you're going to play partner for a diamond honour, it can hardly cost to start with the king.'

The explanation had the desired effect. If the game would take me no farther, it had at least taken us from Calcutta to Delhi.

The story of our international bridge career would probably have ended there if fate hadn't seen fit to play a hand. The World Bridge Federation decided to increase the number of zones. Pakistan would now fall under a new zone known as 'Asia and the Middle East'. Our guardian angel had worked the miracle we needed. Not only would we no longer have to forfeit to Taiwan, but also the new group would be much weaker than the previous one. We would in effect just have to beat India, always a distinct possibility, to qualify for the Bermuda Bowl. No more walkovers!

And that came to pass soon after at the championships in Bangalore, India. We narrowly beat the Indian team and qualified to play in Rye, New York, in the 1981 Bermuda Bowl.

7

Pros and Cons

Atlantic City, Monday Evening: Dinner

I arrived in the lobby to find our dinner group had swelled slightly, from our original three – Tim, the Weasel and myself – we had become eight. All welcome contributors to the standard dinner conversation at all bridge tournaments: the post-mortem of hands.

If you walk into a normal Chinese restaurant, you expect to hear the click of mishandled chop-sticks and familiar references to Shark's Fin Soup and Peking Duck. If you see the diners staring at pieces of paper, the odds are that they are reading about their futures from the fortune cookies.

If you silently agree with the above scenario, I can bet you've never eaten in a Chinese restaurant when there's a bridge tournament in the area. Now the mouths full of Chow Mein splutter out indignant protests as to why their owners led back a heart instead of a spade. The more genteel occupants gulp down huge swallows of Chinese beer to leave their mouths free to dissect some intricate bidding sequence while others, hands still wet with hoisin sauce leaking from the duck pancakes, grab hold of pieces of paper which don't contain their horoscopes but the hand records of the session they have just finished.

The usual practice is to take a few minutes ordering the dinner, then to spend a few hours going over every hand played during the day. The diners usually try hard to linger over the hands where they shone, and to stuff their mouths with Szechuan chicken or other delicacies when their less distinguished moments are about to be spotlighted.

These post-mortems are great – but not only for the fun of reminiscing. They can actually be of enormous benefit to any standard of player, an opportunity to learn and improve. And there is no limit to improvement. An expert can learn something from a beginner, as much as from another expert. There's nothing demeaning in this fact. In bridge, *ego* is sometimes useful, but *hubris* is too dangerous a luxury. If a player listens to the views of others at these sessions, if he carefully registers and records his errors, listing them under category and type, he will improve.

I know several members of the once famous but now defunct Aces team, which was formed by Ira J. Corn, Junior, a Texas oil-baron, to recover the World Championship from the Italians. After every match, they used their post-mortems as self-teaching forums. They had a system of marking their errors. They would put each mistake into one of seven brackets, their Seven Deadly Sins:

1 No-win declarer-play: dumb dummy-play.
2 No-win defence: indefensible strategy.
3 Unilateral bidding: solo flights of fancy.
4 Overbidding: freefall parachute jumping without a rip-cord.
5 Technical errors: the computer blew a fuse.
6 System violation: the amnesia syndrome.
7 Impulsive bidding: the matador without a cape.

I think it is useful to keep a record of your errors. You will soon discover your individual strengths and weaknesses, which probably will be concentrated in specific areas. Each person is different. Maybe your slam bidding lets you down; or your opening leads; or your competitive bidding – even all three. You can only cure something you have diagnosed, which is why I am stressing this point. What was good enough for the Aces is good enough for the world. Anything that gets you to analyse your results cannot help but be beneficial.

Meanwhile, back at the restaurant, someone asked the Weasel what the police (the Tournament Director) was doing at his table in the afternoon. The Weasel was already breaking doctor's orders by eating a spicy beef dish when he was meant to be on a diet. But at the time I thought he may not live to have a heart attack because it was probable that he would burst a blood vessel before he finished the story he was excitedly telling us.

'Who says these players are experts?' he screamed. 'They're fools; they're beginners. Even my daughter could play better.' The Weasel had the attention of the table.

'I am playing with a lady whom I've never seen before, and hope I'll never see again. I've been nice to her and agreed to play all the conventions she wants, even though most of them aren't fit for discussion, let alone playing. In return for playing her way, I tell her that all I want her to do is to try not to revoke and to follow my signals. If I play a high card, she should continue; if I play low, she should switch. Isn't that really simple?'

Immediately I thought that if it had been 'really simple' to the lady in question, we wouldn't have been hearing this, but like the others, I nodded agreement, eager to hear the end of the tale.

'We end up defending four hearts. *She* leads the king of spades. I play the two, hoping for a club switch. *She* continues with another spade. Declarer plays a diamond, which *she* wins with the ace. I play the two, begging for a club switch, but *she* continues a diamond. When she got in yet again with a trump, she still wouldn't play a club, allowing the declarer to make his impossible contract.'

The Weasel was turning a strange shade of purple. Worried about his blood pressure, I made him take a drink of water to calm down. Someone else took over the story.

'Suddenly everyone started yelling for the police, claiming the Weasel had gone berserk. He had torn his cards into pieces and thrown them away. The director asked him if it was true that he had torn up his cards, and if he had anything to say in his defence.

'The Weasel replied that he had indeed torn up his cards, but maintained that he was under such provocation that he had to choose between murdering his partner and tearing his cards. With only those choices, what else could he do? Surely a case of justifiable tearing! The director, who used to be a player, understood the situation and admonished the Weasel's partner to defend better next time!'

At this everybody broke into peals of laughter, and even the Weasel recovered enough to grin.

Upon returning to the hotel I saw Paul Chemla, the French player, walking sadly around the casino floor, muttering unintelligible French words to himself. When I asked him why he was following this odd pattern, he announced with his usual exaggeration that he wished he had never come to America and was seriously contemplating suicide.

'Everybody kills me all day. First as partners they don't know how to take a finesse, and then as opponents they misbid and end up in a ridiculous contract, which they make thanks to a miraculous lie of the cards. To make matter even worse, the food is horrible, and the croupiers at the blackjack table hate me and take all my money. What else is there for me to do except commit suicide?'

Chemla is a very bright guy, and a disciplined and controlled bridge player. Yet somehow like many other disciplined people in and out of the bridge world, he can't resist an undisciplined flutter at the tables. His gambling losses are legendary. In fact he flutters with his money until he has nothing left to flutter. I find it amazing the way gambling can totally influence, even change, a person's character. I admit to being undisciplined in the casino, but at least I am consistent and play bridge the same way.

It's a sort of Jekyll & Hyde syndrome that is difficult to explain. Changing the subject, I asked him about the French team for the World Championships. France and Brazil are the only bridge nations that have any claim to challenging the supremacy of the Americans at the international level. France has eight to ten of the very best players, but rivalries and differences mean that they rarely play together. The Americans have 80 to 100, and so have less difficulty in putting together a good team. Most other nations have no more than two world-class players.

Chemla normally changes his partners like other people their ties, but his present *confrère*, Michel Perron, is top class and unflappable, which is crucial for playing with Chemla. Earlier in his career, Chemla had partnered Michel Lebel, who is more temperamental though a great player. I remember a board, in different rooms, on which both Chemla and Lebel played brilliantly. It came up during the Rosenblum Teams at the Miami Olympiad in 1986.

Dlr: South
Vul: Love All

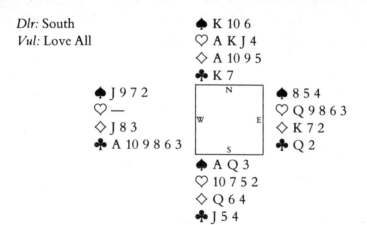

♠ K 10 6
♡ A K J 4
◇ A 10 9 5
♣ K 7

♠ J 9 7 2
♡ —
◇ J 8 3
♣ A 10 9 8 6 3

♠ 8 5 4
♡ Q 9 8 6 3
◇ K 7 2
♣ Q 2

♠ A Q 3
♡ 10 7 5 2
◇ Q 6 4
♣ J 5 4

In Miami there was a Vu-Graph presentation. The game at one table was displayed on a large screen, the bids and plays being relayed through from the closed room. Commentators analysed the deal as play progressed.

West	North	East	South
			Chemla
			Pass
Pass	1 ◇	Pass	1 ♡
Pass	3NT[1]	Pass	4 ♡
Pass	Pass	Pass	

[1] A balance raised to four hearts.

With the trumps breaking 5–0 offside, four hearts looked near-impossible. But Chemla made the contract in about 40 seconds! He won the low spade lead in the dummy with the king, then cashed the ace of hearts, getting the bad news. Chemla took his two spade winners before leading a diamond to the ten and king. East returned a diamond, declarer winning in hand with the queen. Chemla led a club to the king, cashed the ace of diamonds, and led the last diamond, ruffed by East and overruffed by South. That left this position:

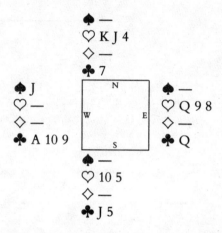

```
                    ♠ —
                    ♡ K J 4
                    ◇ —
                    ♣ 7
         ♠ J                    ♠ —
         ♡ —           N        ♡ Q 9 8
         ◇ —       W       E    ◇ —
         ♣ A 10 9     S         ♣ Q
                    ♠ —
                    ♡ 10 5
                    ◇ —
                    ♣ J 5
```

Chemla exited with a club, which West won with the ace in order to lead another club. East was able to overruff the dummy, but then had to lead from his queen-nine of hearts into dummy's king-jack. Plus 420.

In the Closed Room, this was the auction:

West	North	East	South
		Lebel	
			Pass
Pass	1 ♣[1]	1 ♡	Dble[2]
2 ♣	3 ♣[3]	Pass	3NT
Pass	Pass	Pass	

[1] Precision: sixteen-plus points
[2] Negative
[3] Asking for a club stopper for notrump

Defending against three notrumps, West led the ten of clubs. We are all told to play third hand high. As a general rule, this is a good one; but it takes a great player to find the right time to break the rule. Here, Lebel was East. When dummy played low, so did he! Declarer could have made the contract by ducking, but naturally he won with the jack. When a heart finesse lost to East, Lebel returned the queen of clubs, his partner overtook with the ace and cashed four more club tricks.

Here is another example of the same principle when defending against a notrump contract:

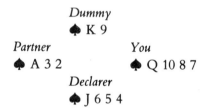

Dummy
♠ K 9
Partner   *You*
♠ A 3 2   ♠ Q 10 8 7
Declarer
♠ J 6 5 4

You know from the bidding that declarer has four spades. When partner leads the suit, if you capture dummy's nine with the queen, you may get only two tricks in the suit. But if you cover the nine with the ten, you get three tricks.

Chemla wasn't in the mood to discuss bridge hands, and headed back towards the blackjack table. I decided to have an early night and carefully avoided the usual group of experts still carrying out post-mortems. This was not so much to be fresh for the bridge tomorrow, but because we had a foursome of golf at the ridiculously early hour of 8.30 a.m.

The 'Pros'

In most sports, like golf, football or athletics, being a professional is an achievement, signifying that the person is good enough to make a living from his skills. Professionals earn respect and fortunes in their chosen fields.

For some reason, bridge is a different story. I doubt there are any professional bridge players in Britain – meaning players who actually live off the game. For a reason I still haven't understood, in a bridge club the biggest insult you can pay someone is to call him a professional. It is a word used scathingly to describe a player who wins regularly.

This is somewhat ironic as I've never met anyone who played to lose. It's true that you don't need to play bridge for money to enjoy the game, but if you do play for a stake, then naturally you want to win. True, some players expect to lose and don't mind doing so too much. But surely everyone prefers the pleasure of winning, and, in my experience, the more you win, the greater the pleasure. Anyone who denies this is probably fooling himself.

In North America, however, there are true professionals. They don't risk their own money at the rubber-bridge table; instead, they compete on the tournament circuit. They are paid fees by their partners, clients who want to learn more about the game or who wish to win. The top pros earn a good living in this way.

Why are the Americans by far the best players in the world today? This 'play for pay' is one reason. The top American players can afford to devote themselves full-time to bridge, and in any sport it is nearly always impossible for amateurs to compete successfully against professionals.

Watching the good players taught me a lot; with perhaps the best lesson being that the biggest winners weren't always the best technical players. Rubber bridge isn't a game, it's a way of life. It is most important to have the mentality of a winner.

Having said that, only a special kind of person can win regularly – unless, of course, he only ever plays with technically far inferior players. To beat your equals or near-equals requires a special sort of thinking, one that I needed to master. I started observing the experts whom I had encountered, and there were many to learn from.

To give you some examples, first there was Terence Reese, arguably the best player ever, and without doubt the best writer. There is a story that his concentration level is so fierce that he did not notice a naked woman walking around his table while he was playing a difficult contract.

With firm views on every subject, a dry, sarcastic humour that is very British, and a brilliant mind, Reese is excellent company. Sadly, by the time I was playing rubber bridge regularly in London, his interest in the game was waning, and to ascertain his opinion on a bidding problem usually required slipping him the question on a piece of paper while he was playing backgammon. His strengths were his logical mind and faultless technique, but he was also a practical player, who comfortably dealt with reality when required.

In his book *Reese on Play*, Terence, playing South, needed to locate a missing queen in this hand:

Dlr: South
Vul: Game All

      ♠ A 6 4
      ♡ A 7 5
      ◇ Q J 9 5 3
      ♣ 4 3

      ♠ K Q J
      ♡ K J 10
      ◇ K 10 6 2
      ♣ A K 7

West	North	East	South
			2NT
Pass	3 ◇	Pass	3NT[1]
Pass	6NT	Pass	Pass
Pass			

[1] With a minimum and only one ace, didn't show any enthusiasm for diamonds.

Reese won the club lead, drove out the ace of diamonds, and won the club return. Now he had to find the queen of hearts to make his contract.

He tried a 'dry run'. First he led the jack of spades from his hand. His left-hand opponent fidgeted slightly – obviously trying to mislead Reese into thinking he had the queen – and then played low. He won with dummy's ace of spades, and returned to hand with a diamond.

Now, aware of his opponent's habits, he attacked the heart suit, leading the jack. This time Reese's left-hand opponent played low smoothly, so Reese finessed – successfully.

We've all been in games where a player hesitates with a singleton, or pretends to have a problem when he doesn't. This sort of behaviour is actually a mild form of cheating. In a tournament you can call the director, but in a more casual game at home, the culprit is often allowed to get away with it.

Maybe one day they'll know better, but meanwhile you should take advantage. The next time you've cut out of a rubber, don't wander away but *watch the game*. Focus closely not just on the bidding and play, but the *manner* in which people bid and play their cards. If they are going to play poker on the bridge table, find out their style and use it against them.

However, remember two things: first, you mustn't look at even the backs of the opponent's cards when you're playing. Second, you must never take advantage of your partner's hesitations; but you may take advantage of your opponents' hesitations – though you do it at your own risk.

Boris Schapiro, Reese's ex-partner, is volatile and opinionated, but very colourful and never boring. Today he is a young man in his eighties, still playing bridge regularly. He finished an amazing second in the 1991 Sunday Times Invitation Pairs Tournament, an event of the very highest standard. He was wont to play with his poodle, Vodka, resting on his lap, but, as his partners will tell you, his bidding was very un-poodle-like. From Boris I learnt that bridge is also a game played with heart and feeling.

Jeremy Flint, who died in November 1989, was at the top of British bridge for almost thirty years. He was a qualified lawyer, and on occasion used his training to think his way out of difficult situations.

He once held this hand:

♠ – ♡ 2 ◇ A K Q J 10 9 7 6 4 3 ♣ K 2

He was partnered with a notorious overbidder, who opened four spades, which traditionally could show any sort of garbage with a seven or eight-card suit.

Flint, naturally, wanted to play in five diamonds, but bidding a minor at the five-level would be taken as a cue-bid, agreeing spades. That was out, but Blackwood was a possibility. If his partner responded five diamonds to four notrumps, he could pass. But there was too great a chance that the response would be five clubs and the situation would worsen. Flint found an ingenious solution. Can you work out how he solved his insoluble problem?

Improvisation is often necessary, so while you are thinking about that, here's another one on a similar theme.

You're non-vulnerable against vulnerable opponents. Your partner opens one heart, and you're holding this sorry collection:

♠ 8 2 ♡ K 7 6 3 ◇ 7 5 2 ♣ 9 8 3 2

It is true that if you judged to pass at this point, you would escape criticism. But you've had a few glasses of Château Lafite '45 at dinner, and you're playing against your least favourite opponents. Still slightly tipsy, you mischievously psych a one-spade response! OK? OK. Partner takes you seriously and raises to three spades. How can you try to extricate yourself from this rather embarrassing turn of events?

Here are the 'answers', but remember they're not 100 per cent guaranteed to work.

On the first hand, with the ten solid diamonds, Flint cue-bid five clubs! Partner was bound to have a singleton or void diamonds. As expected, his partner cue-bid five diamonds. Flint coolly passed. Now you can follow the logic – or lack of it.

On the second hand, cue-bid four diamonds (holding your breath and uttering a silent). Partner will often save you with a cue-bid of four hearts.

There were also the rebels. There are countless stories about the legendary John Collings, perhaps the greatest 'flair' (or natural) player of all time.★ He was also one of the greatest overbidders. I remember that, in particular in fourth chair, he would open three notrumps with any kind of hand, balanced or unbalanced, weak or strong. You never had any idea what he held, and – most annoying of all – he had a habit of making the contract!

★The technical player always looks for the right percentage play, basically ignoring the vibes at the table. A natural player is far more interested in using his table presence. Sometimes he will apparently play against the odds when he is sure it is right to do so. In my opinion, a natural player will normally be a bigger winner than a technician.

I'm sure if I told you that once he bid and made seven hearts missing the K-Q-10-7-5 of hearts, you wouldn't believe me. But it is true: here's how it happened:

Dlr: South
Vul: North–South

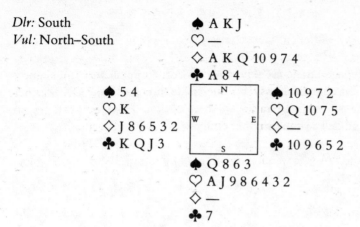

```
                    ♠ A K J
                    ♡ —
                    ◇ A K Q 10 9 7 4
                    ♣ A 8 4
        ♠ 5 4            N           ♠ 10 9 7 2
        ♡ K                         ♡ Q 10 7 5
        ◇ J 8 6 5 3 2  W    E       ◇ —
        ♣ K Q J 3                   ♣ 10 9 6 5 2
                         S
                    ♠ Q 8 6 3
                    ♡ A J 9 8 6 4 3 2
                    ◇ —
                    ♣ 7
```

West	North	East	South
			Collings
			Pass
Pass	2 ♣	Pass	2 ♡
Pass	4NT	Pass	5 ◇
Pass	7 ◇	Pass	Pass
Dble	Pass	Pass	7 ♡
Dble	Pass	Pass	Pass

Collings trusted his partner the first time when he passed seven diamonds. But when West doubled, he retreated to his own eight-card heart suit.

Against this 'impossible' grand slam, West led the king of clubs. Collings won with dummy's ace, then led the ace of diamonds. East ruffed with the five of hearts, so Collings overruffed with the six. Over to dummy with a spade to the king, Collings calling for the king of diamonds, East ruffing with the seven of hearts and declarer overruffing with the eight.

Back to dummy with another spade, Collings led the queen of diamonds. Once more, East ruffed low, this time with the ten of hearts. Collings overruffed with the jack, then cashed the ace of hearts, collecting the king and queen.

'We were lucky the trumps split,' quipped Collings.

His operations were not always successful. Collings had a penchant for passing distribution hands, entering the bidding later at the four- or five-level. Once he passed this hand:

♠ A K Q J 10 7 6 4 3 2 ♡ 5 ◇ 7 ♣ 4

The bidding continued Pass–Pass–Pass! Collings asked his partner what he held. The reply was, 'Just three bare aces.'

Then there is the lovable if roguish Scot, Irving Rose. He made his bids in Cockney rhyming slang, as unintelligible to me now as then. Two of the expressions he used were 'monkey' and 'carpet' (500 and 800, respectively), terms borrowed from horse-racing.

He is another flair player with a great nose for what is happening at the table. I remember the time I saw him holding this hand:

♠ 4 ♡ 9 8 2 ◇ K Q J 10 8 7 5 4 ♣ 2

Non-vulnerable against vulnerable, his partner opened three clubs, promising – under their agreement – two of the top three honours. The next player overcalled four spades. What would you bid now?

Rose jumped to six clubs! He was planning, of course, to run to six diamonds if doubled. But the next player, sure his partner was short in clubs, took the bait and bid six spades.

This came back to Rose, and he added insult to injury by doubling. He was taking the 2 to 1 on chance that his partner had the ace of clubs. Rose led his singleton club, partner did win with the ace and did return the suit for Rose to ruff. With apologies to Cyrano de Bergerac, that's what I call a *nose*!

He hasn't lost his touch. As recently as 1990, in the Netherlands Rose held this hand:

♠ 4 ♡ 9 ◇A Q J 7 6 ♣ K J 10 8 4 3

His partner opened one spade, his right-hand opponent overcalled four hearts, and he was faced with a problem of how to find the right minor suit (4NT would be Blackwood).

For him, the solution was simple – what else but bid four spades! He was sure the opponents would double, and then he could bid four notrumps – again unusual – and find the better minor-suit fit. His plan backfired when four spades was passed out! But his genius was not lacking because four spades made! This type of play was the kind I found most exciting. I revelled in pulling off a 'coup' over the opponents, often ignoring the many losses I incurred to get there. It was always the lure of the open beautiful moment that lay waiting in the wings.

Hoffman is another memorable player. Martin is one of the best card players I have ever seen. He has to be, to make up for his eternal losing streak on the dogs and horses. He has had an amazing life, having been rescued from Auschwitz at the age of eight and brought to England. Without any formal education, he took up bridge; he's another natural. Hoffman plays quicker than anyone else I have ever seen. His only drawback is that his bidding is very optimistic. I remember this conversation after a matchpoint event:

'Martin, what was your score on board thirty-five?'

'Minus fifty,' came Hoffman's reply.

Yes, everyone seems to have gone down in four spades. Couldn't it be made?'

'Four spades? Oh, no, I went one down in *six* spades. I couldn't make *that*!'

That was his way, playing a contract two levels higher than everyone else but taking two more tricks for an average.

Hoffman was a master of inducing errors from his opponents. Suppose you are looking at this everyday holding:

Dummy
♠ 9 8 2

Declarer
♠ A K 7 6 5

How do you play the suit wanting to make as many tricks as possible?

Most players would incorrectly start with the ace. No matter how sweet-natured you are, if you're a bridge player, you love making the opponents look foolish. Perhaps you cash the ace and king, hoping for a 3–2 break. But you would do better to lead the nine from the dummy.

This might be the layout:

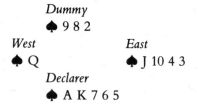

Dummy
♠ 9 8 2

West　　　　　　　　*East*
♠ Q　　　　　　　　♠ J 10 4 3

Declarer
♠ A K 7 6 5

East might be tempted to cover with the ten, whereupon you will lose no trick instead of one, later finessing East out of his jack. The principle is always to start by leading the highest card possible from the short hand, tempting a cover.

Of course, if East plays low, you put up the ace. When the queen appears, it is correct to continue with a low spade to the eight, preparing for a finesse against East's remaining honour if the suit is breaking 4–1.

Similarly:

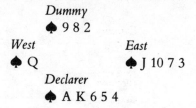

Dummy
♠ 9 8 2

West   East
♠ Q   ♠ J 10 7 3

Declarer
♠ A K 6 5 4

If you lead the nine from the dummy and East covers with the ten, you will lose only one trick instead of two.

How about the embarrassment the opponents will feel if you make a small slam missing the ace, king and ten of trumps. Impossible, you say? Maybe, maybe not.

Look at this deal:

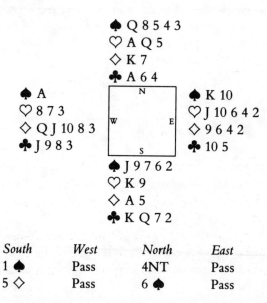

♠ Q 8 5 4 3
♡ A Q 5
◇ K 7
♣ A 6 4

♠ A   ♠ K 10
♡ 8 7 3   ♡ J 10 6 4 2
◇ Q J 10 8 3   ◇ 9 6 4 2
♣ J 9 8 3   ♣ 10 5

♠ J 9 7 6 2
♡ K 9
◇ A 5
♣ K Q 7 2

South	West	North	East
1 ♠	Pass	4NT	Pass
5 ◇	Pass	6 ♠	Pass

You opened the bidding with one spade – clearly a mistake, because partner wouldn't stop bidding – worse, East is 'The Teacher'. You'll never hear the end of it.

You're in six spades, so you might as well try to make it. Naturally, after winning the queen-of-diamonds lead in the dummy, leading a low spade won't help. Your best chance is to call for the queen of spades. Maybe East will cover with the king, maybe even the teacher.

Similarly:

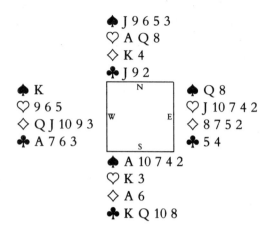

♠ J 9 6 5 3
♡ A Q 8
◇ K 4
♣ J 9 2

♠ K
♡ 9 6 5
◇ Q J 10 9 3
♣ A 7 6 3

N
W   E
S

♠ Q 8
♡ J 10 7 4 2
◇ 8 7 5 2
♣ 5 4

♠ A 10 7 4 2
♡ K 3
◇ A 6
♣ K Q 10 8

Again in six spades with a definite loser in clubs and a possible trump loser, lead the jack of spades from the dummy. A friendly East will cover with the queen.

Sometimes you might need to paint an inaccurate picture in a defender's mind.

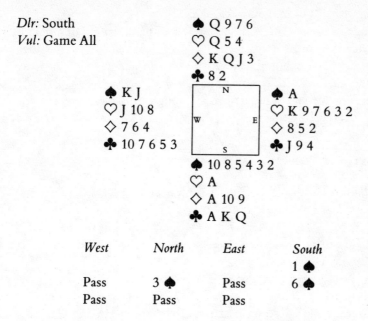

Dlr: South
Vul: Game All

	♠ Q 9 7 6	
	♡ Q 5 4	
	◇ K Q J 3	
	♣ 8 2	

♠ K J	N	♠ A
♡ J 10 8	W E	♡ K 9 7 6 3 2
◇ 7 6 4		◇ 8 5 2
♣ 10 7 6 5 3	S	♣ J 9 4

	♠ 10 8 5 4 3 2	
	♡ A	
	◇ A 10 9	
	♣ A K Q	

West	North	East	South
			1 ♠
Pass	3 ♠	Pass	6 ♠
Pass	Pass	Pass	

You really must do something about your bidding. Once more you get too high and you see your opponents have two guaranteed trump tricks. West leads the jack of hearts. To make the hand, you need to find both the ace and king of spades as singletons – or to induce a defensive error. Can you do anything to encourage such an error?

The best chance is to cover the jack-of-hearts lead with the queen, capturing East's king with your ace. Next, cash the ace of diamonds; then lead a low spade.

Thinking that the ace of diamonds was a singleton, some Wests *might* rise with the king of spades to cash his heart winner before you take a pitch on dummy's diamonds. Again the most important point is that *they won't go wrong if you don't help them a little.*

There is a corollary of this type of play. In 1989 I entered a tip in the annual Bols Bridge Tips competition run by the International Bridge Press Association. The gist of my tip was this: *When they don't cover an honour, they don't have it.*

If an honour isn't covered, declarer should place the key higher honour in the other hand. But there are a few provisos:

1   The length must be in the concealed hand.
2   The declarer should not be known to have special length or strength in the suit.
3   The honour in the dummy should not be touching another: the jack, not the queen-jack, for example.
4   The pips in the suit should be solid enough to make it possible for you to overtake your honour without costing a trick when the suit breaks badly.

This was a typical example:

Dlr: South
Vul: East–West

♠ K Q 3 2
♡ A 4 3
♢ J 4
♣ K J 6 5

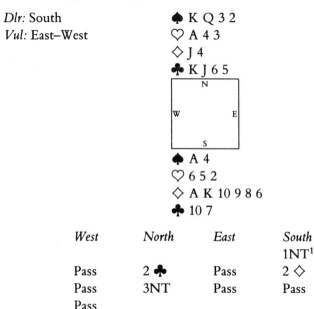

♠ A 4
♡ 6 5 2
♢ A K 10 9 8 6
♣ 10 7

West	North	East	South
			1NT[1]
Pass	2 ♣	Pass	2 ♢
Pass	3NT	Pass	Pass
Pass			

[1] 12–14 points.

You decide to start with a slightly offbeat one notrump: West leads the seven of hearts, and you win the third round in the dummy. Now you call for the jack of diamonds. When East plays low smoothly, it is likely he doesn't have the queen, so put up the king and cash the ace, bringing down the queen and claiming ten tricks.

Here is the layout:

Dlr: South
Vul: E–W

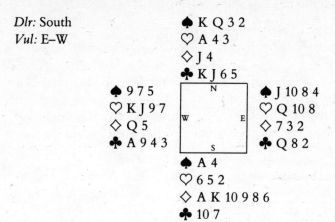

♠ K Q 3 2
♡ A 4 3
◇ J 4
♣ K J 6 5

♠ 9 7 5
♡ K J 9 7
◇ Q 5
♣ A 9 4 3

♠ J 10 8 4
♡ Q 10 8
◇ 7 3 2
♣ Q 8 2

♠ A 4
♡ 6 5 2
◇ A K 10 9 8 6
♣ 10 7

The percentage addicts would finesse the jack of diamonds and go down.

Roll over, Houdini, the magicians are coming!

8

Swing High, Swing Low

I was introduced to golf by the crazy Italian bridge superstar, Benito Garozzo. Immediately I became addicted. I foolishly bet him that I would beat him playing off a fifteen handicap after a year at the game (he plays off twenty-four). Me and my big mouth. In spite of the help of an attractive lady golf pro whose swing was irresistible, I lost the bet.

I find a lot of similarities in golf and bridge. In both games the right mental attitude and confidence can work to help you perform better, physically or mentally. The major difference is the attitude of players towards each other. Bridge once had the image of a refined game for gentle people – but no more. The popular conception is now of two furious people tearing each other's hair out. Sadly, this is too often a true depiction. It seems it's easy to forget that the aim is enjoyment for everyone. Bridge partners, especially good players, are not meant to bully weaker ones. Yet they do.

This is not so in golf, where good players invariably take time out to encourage, advise and sympathize with the 'hackers'. Golf is a very humbling experience; it's difficult to be arrogant when you can't hit the ball. So if you have an unsympathetic bridge partner, try taking him out on the golf course. He might learn a lesson.

When I started playing and reading about bridge, I dreamt about partnering one of the great players, perhaps even one of the legendary Blue Team. It had never occurred to me that the partnership would be on the golf course. But that morning I was playing with Garozzo.

Disaster: we played badly and lost comfortably. Garozzo is as famous for his competitive nature as his temper, and I spent my time avoiding his barrage of choice Neapolitan abuse as well as his hurled golf clubs. If nothing else, the outing enriched my vocabulary of Italian slang.

I was happy to get back to the hotel, to the safety of the one-armed bandits. They only wanted to rob me, not kill me. But at least I was ready to play bridge. Game time was 1 p.m. and we were well in time. The second day of the qualifying stage is different from the first in that people near the top of the field try to maintain their positions by playing down the middle and avoiding risks, while those at the back of the pack start 'swinging' a little, hoping to make up the lost ground.

Swinging is a term used in duplicate bridge to describe taking unusual actions. The theory is that a poorly placed player can only make up ground by doing something different from the leaders. Swinging, more often than not, ends up unsuccessfully, being by definition anti-percentage bridge. Often swinging and overbidding are closely related, and the natural tendency is to go to extremes. This is manifested by actions like doubling too much, pre-empting wildly, and overbidding to hopeless contracts when holding unsuitable hands. The result of such 'hyper-action' more often than not is that the practitioner falls even further behind.

However, sensible swinging, if that isn't a paradox, can be an art, entailing subtlety and psychology rather than brute force. Here are a few suggestions that should prove useful in various forms of duplicate.

1   In a team match, the leading team often 'anticipates' that the other team will come out swinging, and decides to keep pace by overbidding also. Fool them: go the other way, playing conservatively, even underbidding in close situations.
2   Play different methods from your competition as far as possible. For example, if the opponents use a 15–17 one-notrump opening bid, try playing 12–14, the weak notrump. Your results will automatically vary.

While doing this, try to work out what will be happening at the other tables. For example, you pick up:

♠ A 9 5　♡ Q 8 5 4　♢ –　♣ Q 10 9 7 6 3

Your partner opens with a weak notrump. How do you plan the auction?

If the field is playing a strong notrump, at other tables, the bidding will begin instead with one club or one diamond. And if there is a 4–4 heart fit, this will be located immediately. But if you are looking for a swing, you would do better to give up on the heart fit. Instead, bail out into three clubs by whichever method you employ. You can be sure few pairs will have reached this contract.

If, however, the field is using the weak notrump, you have an alternative swinging action. There, most pairs will remove to three clubs. You should use Stayman, hoping to uncover a 4–4 heart fit. If the heart fit doesn't come to light, you can pass if he rebids two spades over Stayman; or you can bid two notrumps (or three clubs, if you play that as non-forcing) over two diamonds.

3 Swing in the card-playing rather than the bidding. For example, how would you play this suit?

Dummy
♣ K 10 9 4

Declarer
♣ A J 8 5 2

The 'normal' percentage play is to lead out the ace and king, hoping to drop the queen. But you can swing gently by taking a finesse for the queen.

Or how about this one?

Dummy
♣ 8 5 4

Declarer
♣ A K J 7 3

In a more desperate situation, play to drop the doubleton queen offside, instead of taking the finesse like the other declarers.

4 Look for slightly unusual leads that could work out. For example, if you pick up:

♠ Q 9 8 7 ♡ 6 4 3 ◇ K 5 4 ♣ 8 6

On lead against three notrumps after an unrevealing auction of 1 N T–3 N T, try the effect of leading a heart, not the more routine spade.

5 Pre-emptive styles can affect results, so try to adopt a different one from your opponents.

6 Adopt swing tactics like sandbagging, which is the art of bidding slowly with big distributional hands.

Back to the game. That last point makes me wince. I was playing steadily, avoiding the flak from the more desperate competitors, when I picked up this hand:

♠ A 9 4 2 ♡ A J 8 3 ◇ 10 4 ♣ Q 6 2

At unfavourable vulnerability, the auction started like this:

West	North	East	South
			Zia
1 ◇	1 ♠	2 ◇	3 ◇[1]
4 ◇	Pass	5 ◇	?

[1] A limit raise or better – in spades.

What would you do now?

Don't answer. Before you reply to any bridge question like this, always ask who your opponent is. So who was he? OK, I'll tell you. He was Bobby Levin, a James Dean lookalike and a top-class player.

What do you do?

At the table I doubled: a bad action for many reasons, not least of all the result, which was minus 800 (under the new scoring that has been in effect since 1987, awarding a 100-point bonus for making a redoubled contract). East had been at it and I fell right into his trap. He redoubled and then made the contract. This was the full deal:

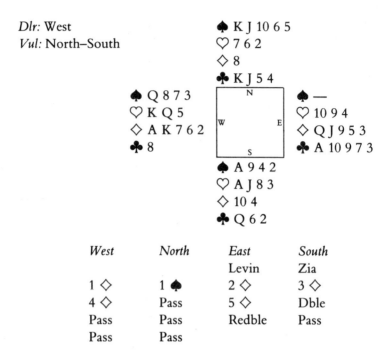

Dlr: West
Vul: North–South

♠ K J 10 6 5
♡ 7 6 2
◇ 8
♣ K J 5 4

♠ Q 8 7 3
♡ K Q 5
◇ A K 7 6 2
♣ 8

♠ —
♡ 10 9 4
◇ Q J 9 5 3
♣ A 10 9 7 3

♠ A 9 4 2
♡ A J 8 3
◇ 10 4
♣ Q 6 2

West	North	East	South
		Levin	Zia
1 ◇	1 ♠	2 ◇	3 ◇
4 ◇	Pass	5 ◇	Dble
Pass	Pass	Redble	Pass
Pass	Pass		

I should never have doubled, but full credit to East. This is a good example of a way in which a player can generate a 'swing'.

Here's a more difficult one.

To set the scene, you're in one of the early rounds of the Vanderbilt (one of the major North American National Team Championships). Your opposition is top class, and with sixteen boards to go, you are trailing by an even 40 imps. The good news is that you have started a rally and feel that with one more good result, you might just be out of trouble. The bad news is there are only two boards to go: you're running out of time. You can never see a void in a hand, but it is always a green light – a chance to get moving.

At favourable vulnerability, sitting East, you pick up this hand.

♠ 10 9 3 2 ♡ 8 2 ◇ – ♣ K Q J 10 9 7 6

The auction starts like this:

West	North	East	South
			1NT[1]
Pass	2 ◇[2]	?	

[1] 15–17 points.
[2] Transfer to hearts.

What do you bid? Most bridge players have a habit of bidding first and thinking later. Your reaction might be to bid anything from three clubs to six clubs. Think ahead – that's what will happen in the other room. But you need a swing. If you jump in clubs, your LHO will pass, RHO will bid his hearts and you will end up on lead against some number of hearts.

But you don't want to be on lead. You want your partner to be on lead so you can ruff a diamond. You must allow your LHO to bid hearts first. The correct bid is pass. Let your LHO bid hearts. Let your RHO bid his game, or slam. Then double for a diamond lead and win the match. Congratulations – you are a swinger.

For most of the session, things went well, and when play finished I was confident that I had qualified. Not in itself such a big deal, but accidents do happen, and a surprising number of top players did fail to make the cut. In fact when the results were posted I had moved up, to a comfortable fifth.

The first step was over. Tomorrow the main event would begin, but for now we could relax. The leaders were mostly familiar names with the majority, perhaps 80 per cent of the 40 qualifiers, being men. However, the few women represented were the best and would hold their own. Why so few women?

That is a delicate question. If you asked the best players to make a list of the top 100 players in the world, today not one of them would include the name of a woman – sad but true. However, the old-timers would have had the US champion Helen Sobel high on their list.

This fact would be agreed to by all the men and even most of the women; today bridge at the top is all men. Why is this? There are two main theories about this. The first, held mainly by women but also by some men, is that women have traditionally not had the same opportunities as men, first by having the time to devote to the game but also because women are conditioned by society to believe that they cannot compete successfully with men. They aren't given the chance to play enough at the top levels. They are not included in the men's teams, and by playing in women's events, as opposed to open tournaments, they aren't given the chance to improve and fulfil their maximum potential. The proponents of this view believe that, given the same opportunities, women could compete to an equally high standard.

The opposing view is that women are 'made' differently from men, their physiological compositions being less suited for whatever it takes to be a top bridge player. Proponents of the second view do not feel that these differences make women less competent than men in other fields, only in specific areas which draw on particular skills: chess and poker being further examples.

I have to agree with the second group. My women friends tell me I am chauvinistic. They are probably right, but I don't think I am being so here. I do genuinely feel that women can perform most intellectual activities as well or even better than men. I believe, for instance, that women's inherent qualities as leaders are undoubtedly at least equal to men. But men and women are different, and the world is not always a logical place when it comes to the sexes.

Perhaps a friend of mine, the reputed psychologist Marty Seligman, has the real answer. He maintains that one of the ingredients that goes into making a top player is the male hormone, testosterone. It is found more in men than in women. This might explain the dilemma. I haven't got the courage to discuss this subject any more – it's far too explosive. But I feel that if argument number one were correct, there would be at least a few isolated instances of a woman being up there with the men.

Be that as it may, it seems that this question will be answered in the near future, because American women bridge players, most unhappy with the status quo, have rebelled.

Jill Blanchard, a top woman player, took the American Contract Bridge League (ACBL) to court to force them to stop holding segregated men's and women's events, and to open up men's events to anyone regardless of sex. An estimated 50 million women bridge players were behind her.

Jill first decided that she wanted to play in open events after the following incident. She was playing with her mother, Gail Greenberg, who is many times a world champion in women's events. They had bid well to a contract of seven clubs. The contract had gone down because of a bad break in a side suit, and Gail told Jill, 'Don't you know you don't bid grand slams in women's events, even if it's the best contract. You get a good enough score just bidding six.'

Gail was right; they scored terribly as no one else had bid to the good grand slam. And if they had bid six, they would have scored over average.

The whole affair infuriated Jill, who thought it was ridiculous that to do well in women's bridge, the recommended action was to play 'badly'. She won the court case, and now in North America there are no tournaments restricted to men. In 1990, by beating the top males, Jill won the right to take part in the play-offs to select the 1991 American Bermuda Bowl world championship team. Her squad contained three men and three women, the first time more than one woman had been on a trials team. They didn't win, but they did a lot to boost women's bridge.

9

Table Presents and Table Presence

Atlantic City, Tuesday Evening

A group of us had dinner in the hotel. Tim hadn't qualified for the final, although the Weasel, still complaining, was comfortably in. But Tim wasn't worried as he had an alternative attraction. He told us over dinner of a backgammon game he had planned for the evening – one of the common perks of tournaments – and of the interesting situation he had fixed.

He would play ten matches of one game each with his opponent. The stake would vary, and the interesting part was that neither of them would know what it was until the game was over. One of them would place a dollar bill under the board before each game. After the game, they would remove the bill; the stake would be for the last four figures on the note. Thus, the stake was a minimum of nothing (usually at least $1000) and a maximum of $9999! No wonder he wasn't too concerned at being out of the final. His opponent was Louie, a successful sports better and bookmaker from New York. Louie was also a fine backgammon player, and was used to big action. The game figured on being good watching, but Louie likes privacy when he plays. We would have to hear later about any presents the players received.

Table Presence

Everyone remembers how they learned to play bridge. Part of that learning process is playing with better players, and I, too, followed this route – paying for the privilege on occasion. And as I progressed, moving up in stakes periodically, perhaps the most important lesson of all that I learnt was not to be involved in the emotion of winning and losing, recognizing that both were inevitable, and that they interfered with judgment. This was a difficulty, but after a while I became almost immune to the results. It is vital to be detached when gambling.

There were other lessons. The top players each had individual traits from which I could learn. They also had common traits, ones that every bridge player should master. To become a complete bridge player, you need a mixture of qualities – some worked for, some acquired, and others innate.

Card sense is the most obvious talent of the 'gifted'. This is an innate ability; but if you aren't born with a body full of card sense, you can still 'learn' about cards. The players with card sense enjoy a familiarity and ease with the cards. Often they 'know' how the cards lie. All the great players have it.

Another quality that is partly innate and partly acquired is *table presence*.

Have you ever known that an opponent was going to make a particular bid even before he made it? Have you ever felt sure that someone, either your partner or an opponent, was about to play a specific card, and he did? Have you ever sensed that a key suit was going to break badly and been right? Or, have you wanted to double the opponents for no good reason, decided against it, and cursed later when they went several down?

It's possible that at each of these times you were using psychic gifts that allow you to look into the future. But it is very unlikely. There may be a place for magic, but it isn't at the bridge table. It is much more likely that, without knowing it, you were using table presence.

For years table presence has been part of the private domain of the expert. It is a mysterious, charismatic quality that allows demigods at the bridge table to dazzle and delight. One moment they locate a missing queen or jack, the next they make an inspired bid in an apparently hopeless situation. And when a mere mortal asked for the explanation of the bid or play, the answer would always be the same: 'table presence'.

Yet nobody has ever explained table presence. What exactly is it? Where do you find it? How do you keep it? Is it catching?

Relax, I am about to tell you. Table presence is simply a term used to describe the way a player knows or feels what's happening around the table. One inch under the atmosphere around every table, there's an invisible screen on which a movie is continually being played. Most people don't know it's there, but the successful player is one who can see it, hear it and feel it.

You are in a grand slam, the moment of truth arrives and you have to guess this combination in order to catch the queen.

Dummy
♠ A 10 4

You
♠ K J 7

Can you recall the tenseness and anticipation around the table? Reading that atmosphere correctly is one of the most valuable talents in bridge. But it isn't easy to come by. There are a few who can really read the table. One of these was P. Hal Sims. He was an American player who boasted that he had never misguessed a two-way finesse for a queen. He would always 'smell' it out, and was prepared to put money where his mouth was. To test him, a friend once 'fixed' a hand, putting Sims into a grand slam in which he had to guess a two-way finesse in spades.

After thinking for some time, Sims leapt out of his chair, shouting, 'This is impossible – you've both got the queen!' And he was right!

Acquiring table presence isn't as difficult as it seems. Suppose declarer opens with a strong notrump and his partner raises to three notrumps. You make a lead and dummy comes down with a thirteen-count.

At this point, on most occasions a defender can relax because the contract is probably going to be easy. But if you see the declarer, who has a minimum of 28 points between the two hands, taking a long time to play, *wake up*. He's obviously got a problem. It's no time to relax. That's table presence.

Say you are the declarer in a four-spade contract that seems to have an easy ten or eleven tricks, yet your left-hand opponent, a capable player, is taking a long time to play. Be careful, probably the suits are breaking badly or there's a ruff lurking and he is planning how to defeat you. That's table presence.

You open one notrump and partner gives you three notrumps. Your left-hand opponent takes a long time to lead. That's already interesting. He's unlikely to have a five-card suit – unless he has a very weak hand with no entry and is trying to find his partner's long suit. Play the hand accordingly. That's table presence.

When an opponent hesitates, you should try to work out why he is pausing (though remember always that you do this at your own risk). However, it is totally impermissible purposely to try to mislead an opponent by hesitating, or to take advantage of information gleaned from your own partner's pause.

A slow raise of an invitation usually means a minimum; a quick raise a maximum. We've all heard happy and sad bids. Often you can tell what your opponent holds. If you haven't been doing it, start registering such information and using it. This is another example of table presence. Feeling the mood of your opponent, and trying to understand what he's thinking and why, are winning tactics. It can look magical at times, too.

Once I was playing against a top expert in an international event. He thought for several seconds longer than usual before opening one no-trump. I scribbled on a piece of paper: 'Your distribution is 2-4-5-2.'* His mouth fell open in amazement!

I hadn't peeped at his hand, and I'll admit I was a bit lucky. Here's how my thoughts went: He's opened one notrump, but there's something unusual about his hand. Most players are strict about their point-count requirements; the likelihood is that he is off-shape. Opening one no-trump with a six-card minor is a common practice. But if that had been his problem, he would have solved it quicker. He is probably some 5-4-2-2, and was debating whether to reverse or to open one notrump. With a five-card major, surely he would open in that suit. So his long suit must be a minor. My hand was:

♠ A J 6 5 ♡ 10 7 ◇ 9 4 ♣ A Q 6 5 2

It was likely he had length in my short suits: i.e. four hearts and five diamonds.

Only slightly to my surprise, my prediction proved to be accurate. But, as you can see, the reasoning wasn't complicated. It was an example of table presence.

Were you ever clutching queen-to-three spades and the opponents bid all the way to seven spades? Can you recall trying to look bored when your partner started to ask a questions about the bidding? No doubt you felt terrible, sure that the questions would alert the declarer who would pick up your queen. No one would ask a lot of questions when looking at the queen of trumps with the opponents in seven.

Well, remember that the next time *you* are the declarer. That's *table presence*.

---

* Two spades, four hearts, five diamonds and two clubs.

Every rule has an exception, and I'm still trying to forget this one from a friendly game. I was holding declarer in seven clubs with this trump suit:

Dummy
♣ A 4 3

Declarer
♣ K J 9 5 2

Not the best grand. The dummy had been tabled and I was about to cash the ace and follow with a finesse of the jack, when my right-hand opponent started asking a string of questions about the bidding. I was sure he couldn't have the queen of clubs. I won the first trick in hand and led the jack of clubs. Wrong! He won with the queen, from queen-to-three. He was just a beginner and genuinely curious about the auction. He hadn't reached the stage where he would become too nervous to ask.

He Who Hesitates is Last

It's hard to list the rules regarding this subject. Every situation is different. The one crucial point is to understand that honest people always hesitate for a reason; your job is to work out why. Try this. After a heavy day at the office, you pick up a goodish hand:

♠ 8 4 ♡ K 6 5 ◇ A 8 3 ♣ A Q J 9 2

There are two passes to you, and though having only fourteen points, you opt to open with a 15–17-point *one notrump* because you like the look of your nine of clubs. Your left-hand opponent, a sweet LOL (Little Old Lady) who always has her bid, overcalls *two spades*.

Partner bids *three spades*, which is Stayman in this sequence. You don't have a spade stopper or four hearts, so you continue with a natural *four clubs*.

After a pass by the LOL, your partner says, 'Points, schmoints and leaps – six clubs!'

In spite of your minimum your hand is beginning to look quite good. LHO passes after a slight pause, and then leads the king of spades. This is what you can see:

Dlr: South
Vul: Love All

♠ 10
♡ A J 9 3
◇ K Q
♣ 8 7 6 5 4 3

♠ 8 4
♡ K 6 5
◇ A 8 3
♣ A Q J 9 2

West	North	East	South
	Pass	Pass	1NT
2 ♠	3 ♠	Pass	4 ♣
Pass	6 ♣	Pass	Pass
Pass			

You're both overbid a little but the dummy is about par, the queen of diamonds being the only wastage. You have lost a spade trick, which makes the trump play crucial. You also have a heart problem!

At trick two West switches to a diamond. You win in the dummy and lead a trump, East naturally contributing the ten. Well, do you finesse or play for the drop?

In the absence of outside information, playing for the drop and finessing are close. The actual percentages are 52 per cent for playing the ace, and 50 per cent for finessing.

What clues do we have?

Let's start with the spade position. West seems to have six or seven to the ace-king-queen because if East had three or four spades to the queen, probably he would have doubled the three-spade cue-bid to show support. That's not much help.

There is not much we can deduce about the rest of the distribution, except perhaps to focus on West's slight pause at the end of the auction. Problems are often best tackled by putting yourself in the place of the other person.

Suppose as West you had something like this:

♠ A K Q 9 7 6 ♡ x x x ◇ x x x ♣ K

What would you do over six clubs? That's easy – you'd pass, and quickly (perhaps pulling your cards closer to your chest). Yes – West would have had no problem if she held the king of clubs. She must have been considering sacrificing, bidding six spades. That surely means she's void in clubs.

Happy that you were awake enough to pick up the pause: you finesse the queen of clubs. As expected, West shows out. Justice is served when the heart finesse is on as well, allowing you to pick up the slam bonus.

This was the full hand:

Dlr: South
Vul: Love All

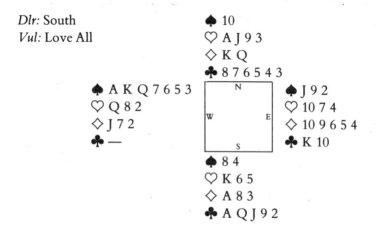

	♠ 10	
	♡ A J 9 3	
	◇ K Q	
	♣ 8 7 6 5 4 3	
♠ A K Q 7 6 5 3	N	♠ J 9 2
♡ Q 8 2	W E	♡ 10 7 4
◇ J 7 2		◇ 10 9 6 5 4
♣ —	S	♣ K 10
	♠ 8 4	
	♡ K 6 5	
	◇ A 8 3	
	♣ A Q J 9 2	

Swedish Delight

Now that you've got the hang of table presence, join me in Stockholm at the 1983 World Championships. As usual you're on centre stage. Sitting South, you pick up a beauty:

♠ A K 2 ♡ A K Q 10 8 ◇ – ♣ A Q 9 7 4

The bidding proceeds:

West	North	East	South
			2 ♣[1]
Pass	2 ◇[2]	Dble[3]	2 ♡
Pass	3 ◇	Pass	4 ♣
Dble	5 ♣	Pass	5 ♠
Pass	6 ♡	Pass	Pass
Pass			

[1] Strong, artificial and forcing.
[2] Negative.
[3] Showing diamonds.

After a confusing auction during which West has asked innumerable questions, your LHO leads the eight of diamonds, which is covered by the jack and king. This is what you can see:

Dlr: South
Vul: Love All

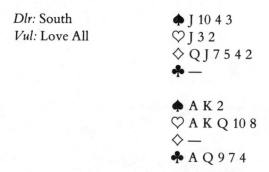

♠ J 10 4 3
♡ J 3 2
◇ Q J 7 5 4 2
♣ —

♠ A K 2
♡ A K Q 10 8
◇ —
♣ A Q 9 7 4

That is a disappointing dummy, but for now your problem is to make six hearts, not to comment on partner's overbidding. What is your plan?

It's a complicated hand, and you probably need the hearts to be 3–2. The 'normal' line must be to cash the ace of clubs, and play to ruff three clubs in dummy. If the king of clubs comes down in three rounds or the clubs are 4–4, you will be home; otherwise you can try the spade finesse.

However, West's double of four clubs and his questions have changed the situation. Remember table presence! Here, when East shows up with the ace-king of diamonds, it becomes likely that West has both missing cards: the king of clubs and queen of spades.

Proceeding in this assumption, you ruff the diamond lead, ruff a club (without cashing the ace), play a spade to the ace, and ruff a second club. A spade to the king is followed by a third club ruff. You trump a diamond in hand, arriving at this position:

♠ J 10
♡ —
◇ Q 7 5 4
♣ —

♠ 2
♡ A K Q
◇ —
♣ A Q

It's time to draw trumps, and West follows to three rounds. Now you exit with your last spade, endplaying West to lead into your ace–queen clubs.

Nicely done! This was the hand:

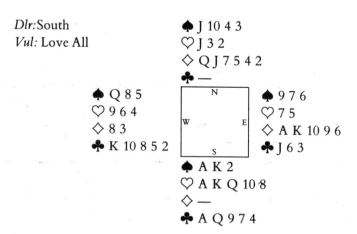

*Dlr:*South
Vul: Love All

♠ J 10 4 3
♡ J 3 2
◇ Q J 7 5 4 2
♣ —

♠ Q 8 5
♡ 9 6 4
◇ 8 3
♣ K 10 8 5 2

♠ 9 7 6
♡ 7 5
◇ A K 10 9 6
♣ J 6 3

♠ A K 2
♡ A K Q 10 8
◇ —
♣ A Q 9 7 4

Playing West for the queen of spades, this line would work even if West started with four spades and only two hearts. He would have been forced to discard his low spade on the third round of hearts.

Another aspect of table presence is anticipating the likely result of the contract. When defending, if you think the contract will make, look for a chance to deflect declarer from the winning line.

You are involved in a tough 64-board match. You've pulled ahead of your opponents, but feel you need one more good board to afford that brandy you've been thinking about. This may be it:

♠ A 8 7 6 4 3 ♡ A K ♢ A K Q 5 ♣ A

You're sitting South, vulnerable against non-vulnerable opponents. This hand, with its long weak suit, is hard enough to bid given a free run – but here West opens with a bid of three clubs. You do what you can, leading to this auction:

West	North	East	South
3 ♣	Pass	Pass	4 ♣[1]
Pass	4 ♡	Pass	5 ♠
Pass	6 ♠	Pass	Pass
Pass			

[1] Indicating a very powerful hand.

West lead the king of clubs, and the dummy comes down to the sniggers of the kibitzers:

Dummy
♠ Q 10 9
♡ 6 5 4 2
♢ 6 3 2
♣ 8 6 5

Declarer
♠ A 8 7 6 4 3
♡ A K
♢ A K Q 5
♣ A

The kibitzers are wrong. At this score, your five spades begged partner to raise with any help. He judged well to bid the slam, but you need something favourable to happen in spades. You win the first trick with the ace of clubs and cash the ace of spades: jack, nine, five. That's revealing – West seems to have started with a singleton spade. You can now test the diamonds, ruffing the fourth round if they don't break. (If East ruffs the third round, you never had a chance.) To your surprise, *West* ruffs the queen of diamonds with the two of spades. This was the hand:

*Dlr:*West
Vul: North–South

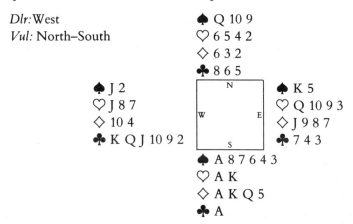

♠ Q 10 9
♡ 6 5 4 2
♢ 6 3 2
♣ 8 6 5

♠ J 2
♡ J 8 7
♢ 10 4
♣ K Q J 10 9 2

♠ K 5
♡ Q 10 9 3
♢ J 9 8 7
♣ 7 4 3

♠ A 8 7 6 4 3
♡ A K
♢ A K Q 5
♣ A

West made a fine play when he threw the jack of spades. Left to your own devices, you would have played the ace and another spade, making when the trumps break 2–2. The false-card was simple yet effective. Most people don't realize that it's often right to drop a high card a round early.

For example, assume that declarer is in a spade contract, and this is the trump layout:

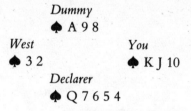

Dummy
♠ A 9 8

West   You
♠ 3 2   ♠ K J 10

Declarer
♠ Q 7 6 5 4

You are entitled to one trick only. If you throw the king of spades under the ace, you'll still get one trick, but South, thinking the suit is breaking 4–1, may abandon trumps and lose another trick later. Similarly:

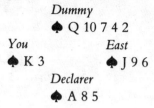

Dummy
♠ Q 10 7 4 2

You   East
♠ K 3   ♠ J 9 6

Declarer
♠ A 8 5

Again, your side is due to get only one spade trick, but if you jettison the king under the ace, declarer might stop playing the suit.

Back in the casino, Sarah Jane seemed to be off duty. Her replacement was an unfriendly man who for some reason annoyed me by the way he pulled the cards out of the shoe. In addition, he belonged to that sadistic clan of croupiers who seem to take great pleasure in winning from the players. He was so unsympathetic that I didn't stay long.

The casino was less lively than the previous day, and I noticed that Omar Sharif was nowhere to be seen. The official word was that he wasn't feeling well, but the inside gossip was that he was unhappy with the casino, and was staying away from the tables.

On the way back to my room, I passed the results board, where a few die-hards were still checking their scores. Errors can occur. In the semi-finals of the World Championship, in Geneva in 1990, the Canadians lost their match to the German team because of a recording error. The German team went on to win the Championship. I tried to think about the next day's play, but I found that the adrenalin hadn't started to flow. I still wasn't into the excitement – there would be time enough tomorrow.

10

Tall Oaks from Little Acorns Grow

Rye Town, New York, October 1981

We had really made it; we had qualified to play in the Bermuda Bowl in Rye, some twenty miles north of Manhattan. We were on a high. The good news was that we were about to participate in our first world championship. The players were excited, and even a few members of the public had started taking an interest in our existence – a good sign. On the down side was the fact that our presence added a new dimension to the meaning of the word 'underdog'. More than a few whispers were heard to the effect that we were bringing down the standard of the event and even that we shouldn't be there. Too bad. It was true that we didn't expect to do well, but the experience had to be good for us, and we hoped that our taking part would promote the game in Pakistan. If nothing else, we could show that we knew a thing or two about sportsmanship.

Everybody was tipping the strong American squad as favourites. They were all new names to us, but that wasn't surprising. Most of the people whose names we would recognize, Culbertson, Goren, and so on, vanished years ago. This time the team included the latest American killing machine: Jeff Meckstroth and Eric Rodwell, two young players reputed to possess an affinity for mercilessly destroying the opposition.

Apart from America, Poland and Great Britain were likely to pose the biggest threat – the British team included some of my rubber bridge friends from the old days in London: Rose, Sheehan and Collings, now enemies at the table. At least I would know how they played when we met them, whatever that would be worth. The rest of the field seemed impressive too, with strong teams from South America and the Far East. No one seemed able even to get our names right, mixing our first and family names almost at random!

The pundits said we had no hope. The journalists said we had no hope. Even the players agreed: no one thought we had any hope – no one except for 'Chance'.

There's an optimist in every group, in every team. Chance was ours. Long ago we called him Chance (his real name is Nisar) because of his adventurous bidding style and never-say-die attitude: no team was too tough for him. The very thought of losing was preposterous.

'Just let me sit at the table against them,' he would assert when the Americans were mentioned. 'I'll deal with them.' Then as proof of what he is capable, he would quote some hand from the past where he pulled off a devilish coup. 'See,' he added confidently, 'I'll make *Keema* (mincemeat) of them.'

I must admit that I liked his attitude, even though his dreams were more fantasy than reality. I could even agree that our players might be able to hold their own in the card-play, but I knew in my heart that that wouldn't be enough.

Bridge had changed in the last decade, especially at the top. Unlike the early days, high-level games had become much more a bidding competition. Highly sophisticated methods had taken over from judgement and card skills. Here we were pitifully outgunned. We were all using old-fashioned Acol, by comparison a simple but antiquated system. Acol is fine for a friendly game at home, but compared to the science of our opponents, it was a bit like fighting nuclear weapons with a bow and arrow. In addition, some of the other players, the Americans, were full-time professionals who played regularly against top-class opposition. We were casual amateurs: a big difference. Our team played irregularly at best.

Where others were preparing vigorously for the competition, combining physical training with twentieth-century technology, even working with computer printouts of their own and their opponents' methods, our group was predictably much more casual. Our biggest challenge seemed to be in making the decision of whether to spend more time buying items like jeans, artificial flowers and other presents on our long shopping lists, or chatting up the women's teams. Objectively I felt that to do well we would need to have a prolonged spell on *Heat 1*.

Do you, as a bridge player, find that on some days you play terribly and on others really well? Have you wondered why? American theorist, Roger Stern, may have the answer. Stern maintains that it is impossible for anyone to play consistently well. We are all bound to play at different levels. There are three main categories, or *heats* as he calls them.

Heat 1

This is the magic heat. You play above yourself. You are no longer a bridge player, you're an artist, a poet. The cards respond to your touch, they fly, they sing, they come alive for you. In addition, everything, luck included, is going for you. You're invulnerable – you can't make a mistake.

Heat 2

This is your normal level or standard. You play as you would expect to: middle of the road.

Heat 3

You wish you'd stayed in bed. You play terribly and out of luck. Every finesse is wrong, every suit breaks badly. The opponents play like champions and you lose, with a capital L.

Stern asserts that if a player can be objective about his heat, he can drastically improve his results. Here's how: each time you play, as soon as possible, carefully determine which heat you are in. Now adjust your game accordingly.

In Heat 1: Get involved, take control, take daring decisions, be strong – remember, you own the table.

In Heat 2: Plod along, do your normal thing.

In Heat 3: Beware, take a back seat. Play passively, play with caution. Whenever possible, let your partner make the key decisions and stay out of the way. Just try to stay alive.

In real life, what normally happens is that when on Heat 3, players invariably try to make up for their bad results. Don't do it – things only get worse. It's almost impossible to think clearly when things are going badly. The trick is to learn not to fight this heat, but to live with it.

Stern's theory is one of the most invaluable pieces of bridge advice ever given to me. I insist that all my partners and team-mates follow it. I would strongly advise bridge players of all levels to use it and watch their results starting improving.

Meanwhile back to the tournament. The format was a double round-robin with the four leading teams after seven days playing off in semifinals and the final. Our group consisted of six players, two officials and just one supporter.

The supporter, Beroze, was unique. Lady bridge supporters are not common in our part of the world, but she's a real enthusiast, and so faithful that she had travelled all the way from Pakistan just to root for us. She never missed a match so it wasn't to be a wasted journey, she needed to have brought a miracle or two along with her.

When the tournament started, for a moment we wondered whether she had come suitably armed because, surprisingly, in the first match we narrowly beat the American giants.

However, we didn't have time for this victory to go to our heads. With a sickening monotony, we lost the next six matches. Disappointed but not too surprised, at the end of the first round-robin, we found ourselves near the bottom of the pack. At the top, the bookies were losing money as Britain and America were leading.

For us, the dreaded Heat 3 seemed to be spreading its poison. Faced with a choice, we invariably did the wrong thing. Here is an example from our seventh-round match against Argentina. At unfavourable vulnerability, I picked up:

♠ Q ♥ A 10 7 6 ◇ K 4 2 ♣ K Q 9 7 6

The auction was difficult:

West	North	East	South
	Masood		Zia
		Pass	1 ♣
1 ♠	3 ◇	4 ♠	4NT[1]
Pass	5 ♣[2]	Pass	5 ♥[3]
Pass	5NT[4]	Pass	7 ◇![5]
Dble[6]	7NT[7]	Pass	Pass
Pass			

[1] Blackwood
[2] Zero or three aces
[3] Asking for extras, according to our system
[4] Undiscussed; just keeping the ball rolling
[5] Hoping for the queen of diamonds and enough bits and pieces
[6] Lightner – he wants a club lead
[7] Knowing that seven diamonds will go down at trick one

West led the king of hearts, and this was what I could see:

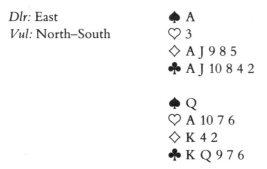

Dlr: East
Vul: North–South

♠ A
♡ 3
♢ A J 9 8 5
♣ A J 10 8 4 2

♠ Q
♡ A 10 7 6
♢ K 4 2
♣ K Q 9 7 6

The key to making the contract was the diamond suit. After winning with the ace of hearts, I took three rounds of clubs, then cashed the king of diamonds: three, five, ten. I played another diamond, West contributing the six. What would you do?

At the time, I couldn't see any reason not to make the percentage play, so I finessed dummy's jack. The roof fell in, as this was the full deal:

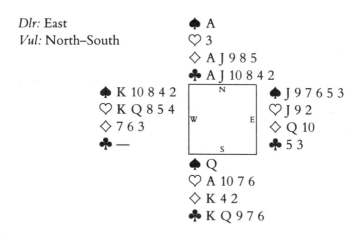

Dlr: East
Vul: North–South

♠ A
♡ 3
♢ A J 9 8 5
♣ A J 10 8 4 2

♠ K 10 8 4 2
♡ K Q 8 5 4
♢ 7 6 3
♣ —

N
W   E
S

♠ J 9 7 6 5 3
♡ J 9 2
♢ Q 10
♣ 5 3

♠ Q
♡ A 10 7 6
♢ K 4 2
♣ K Q 9 7 6

On reflection, I think I made a bad play. West doubled seven diamonds. Yes, he had a club void, but he also knew we might run to seven notrumps. He would certainly have doubled with ♦ 7 6 3, but looking at ♦ Q 6 3 or ♦ Q 7 6 3 he might well have passed over seven diamonds, taking his chance on either getting a club lead anyway or scoring his queen of diamonds. A variation of restricted choice? Or just the kind of hand you need to be on Heat 1 to make?

In the other room, Munir lost 500 in six spades doubled. We dropped fourteen imps on the board, instead of gaining seventeen if I had made the grand. Only 31 imps swinging on a guess.

Our camp was full of long faces. Even Chance was beginning to sound despondent.

Tall Oaks . . .

Help came from the least expected quarter. SAPP (an acronym for Stone-age Acol with Paki Pre-empts) was a bidding system, or so they say. It was the secret weapon and brainchild of Munir, one of our team members. Munir is a Rhodes scholar, and SAPP was a complicated concoction of his brilliant if twisted (trust me) mind.

It works more or less like any other system. Bids at the one-level were old-fashioned Acol, but at the two-level SAPP took its followers into a weird and wonderful world where all bids had multiple meanings. Bids from two clubs to four hearts were all multi-purpose. For instance, an opening bid of three clubs showed either:

- a diamond pre-empt (with a bad suit); or
- a heart pre-empt (with two of the top three honours); or
- a strong 6–4 or 7–4 in spades and hearts; or
- a solid seven-card minor with a king outside; or
- a four-heart or four-spade opener with two first-round controls, one of which may be a void.

I told you his mind was twisted – now maybe you'll believe me.

The original purpose of this system was twofold. First, to drive terror and confusion into the adversaries; and secondly, by playing a method that catered for the 'one-in-a-million' hand, at least we'd gain when – or should I say 'if'? – it came up.

The results so far had been less than spectacular. The good news was that it had succeeded in creating fear and confusion. The bad news was that it filled not his opponents' minds with fear and confusion, but his *partner's* mind! Fazli, Munir's partner, had aged twenty years trying to remember the meanings of all the bids. None of the 'one-in-a-million' hands had come up, so the system hadn't been tried out. Oh we of little faith! Along came this hand:

Dlr: East	♠ A K J 8 7 5 4 3	♠ 9 2
Vul: Game All	♡ 7 6 3	♡ K Q 5
	◇ —	◇ 8 7 4 3
	♣ K 5	♣ A Q 10 7

West	East
Munir	*Fazli*
3 ♣[1]	3 ♡[2]
4 ♠[3]	5 ♣[4]
5 ◇[4]	6 ♠[5]
Pass	

[1] As above: last possibility.
[2] Knowing partner will convert, and prepared to play in four diamonds.
[3] Extra length, a maximum and a slammish hand.
[4] Cue-bid.
[5] Bingo!

Naturally every other human being opened four spades and played there. We picked up a slam swing and won the match. There were two consequences. The first was that Munir was thrilled. For the next few days, he could regularly be found expounding his theories on bidding to anybody who would listen – usually the waitresses in the coffee shop (although there were rumours that he had ulterior motives).

The second consequence was that as if by magic the floodgates opened. Suddenly we were on a roll and the whole team stepped into Heat 1. When an aggressive player gets going, he really goes. Take Chance. At the table, he invented a sequence that even I'd never heard of before – or since. Sitting South, he picked up this hand:

$$♠ 8 3 ♡ A Q 9 ◇ J 10 7 6 4 ♣ A 9 2$$

The bidding went like this:

West	North	East	South
		Pass	Pass
1 ♠	Pass	Pass	Dble[1]
Pass	1NT	Pass	2NT[2]
Pass	3NT[3]	Pass	Pass
Pass			

[1] OK – a normal, protecting double.
[2] The impossible bid: raise à la Chance.
[3] Nishat, Chance's partner, is used to such sequences.

Madness, genius, inspiration – I don't know. I do know that three notrumps made. Heat 1 can be infectious! But first confession time. People think that experts always plan every move or play they make well in advance. They certainly try to, and thinking ahead is fundamental, but the truth is that many times a good declarer or defender just falls into the right line – a mixture of luck and technique. In Heat 1 this happens more frequently than at others. OK, lecture over, try this:

Dlr: South
Vul: East–West

Dummy
♠ 7 2
♡ K J 8 2
♢ 9 4 2
♣ 10 9 4 3

Declarer
♠ A Q 10 6 4
♡ Q 7
♢ K Q J
♣ A Q 8

West	North	East	South
	Masood		Zia
			2NT
Pass	3 ♣[1]	Pass	3 ♠
Pass	3NT	Pass	Pass
Pass			

[1] Stayman.

The match was against the Poles, and the guy on my left, a fine player with an unpronounceable name, led the ten of hearts, showing something or other. I didn't ask, I was too busy trying to form a plan. Anyway, how would you proceed?

Looking at the dummy, my thoughts went like this: 'Not a great contract – the bidding is normal, but the hands fit badly. Where do I start? I'd like to play spades and clubs, at the same time preferably, and both from the dummy, but I am in danger of never getting there.

'It seems likely that West doesn't have a long suit or he wouldn't have led a heart. He knew from the bidding that dummy has four of them. Probably he has honours in the other suits, or he might have been more aggressive.

'This hand is taking too long. As sooner or later I'll have to do something with the spades, I'd better start there. No particular play looks appealing, but if West has the king, leading the queen out of my hand won't cost.'

I played low from the dummy at trick one, as did East, and won in hand with the queen of hearts. I then led the queen of spades, which West won with the king. At least I hadn't wasted my time trying to get into the dummy to take a finesse that was going to lose.

West switched to a diamond, East winning with the ace and returning a second diamond. Next I played a heart to the jack, hoping it might be ducked, but East won with the ace and led a third diamond. From the spots, it looked like he had the thirteenth. With three tricks each, this was the position:

Dlr: South
Vul: East–West

Dummy
♠ 7
♡ K 8
♢ —
♣ 10 9 4 3

Declarer
♠ A 10 6 4
♡ —
♢ —
♣ A Q 8

Now what? Once more, I paused to consider: 'West seems to have started with two hearts, three diamonds and a lot of black cards. With five clubs he would have led one, so he's probably 4–4 or 5–3 in spades and clubs. In either case, playing spades is hopeless. That leaves clubs. If East has the club king, I've no chance, because he'll cash his diamond, so I'll play West for it.

'I still can't see how I'm going to make this hand, but at least I can maintain the symmetry by playing another black queen out of my hand.'

I didn't know it then, but this was the actual position around the table:

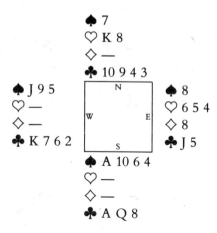

```
                    ♠ 7
                    ♡ K 8
                    ◇ —
                    ♣ 10 9 4 3
    ♠ J 9 5          ┌──────N──────┐      ♠ 8
    ♡ —             │             │      ♡ 6 5 4
    ◇ —          W  │             │  E   ◇ 8
    ♣ K 7 6 2       │      S      │      ♣ J 5
                    └─────────────┘
                    ♠ A 10 6 4
                    ♡ —
                    ◇ —
                    ♣ A Q 8
```

I led the queen of clubs from my hand. To defeat the contract West had to duck his king, but West made a mistake winning the trick. Remember, we were on Heat 1 where opponents do make more mistakes; and East had already erred by failing to hold up his ace of diamonds for two rounds. West played back a club.

It looked as though I had to play low from dummy and hope for a doubleton jack of clubs to win nine tricks. But that wasn't true. There was a much sexier line. I put up the ten of clubs, winning East's jack with the ace. I played a club to dummy's nine, and cashed my two heart winners, squeezing West in spades and clubs. He had to bare his jack of spades, so at trick twelve I led a spade to my ace, dropping his jack!

It looked good and felt great!

This was the full hand:

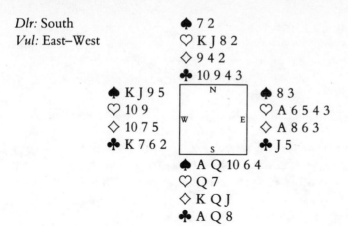

Dlr: South
Vul: East–West

```
                    ♠ 7 2
                    ♡ K J 8 2
                    ◇ 9 4 2
                    ♣ 10 9 4 3
  ♠ K J 9 5          N           ♠ 8 3
  ♡ 10 9                         ♡ A 6 5 4 3
  ◇ 10 7 5      W        E       ◇ A 8 6 3
  ♣ K 7 6 2                      ♣ J 5
                    S
                    ♠ A Q 10 6 4
                    ♡ Q 7
                    ◇ K Q J
                    ♣ A Q 8
```

Boom! We won the next three matches and started gathering in the points, clawing our way up the pack.

We started getting excited.

Some of the spectators started asking, 'Who are these guys?'

We became encouraged enough to start calculating the number of points needed to get to the semifinals.

We actually started listening to our coach.

We even talked about having early nights (just talk; that idea was soon rejected). Actually, early nights in themselves aren't always enough. Anybody who has played enough bridge can tell you that regardless of how exhausted you are, it isn't easy to sleep after a tough game. More likely as you lie in bed, the ghosts of recently played hands come out to haunt you, whirling around inside your consciousness.

First come the most painful deals: the misses – misbids, misplays, missed inferences and mistakes. You curse yourself for your stupidities. If you manage to push these thoughts away, you can then turn your mind to the good moments.

There isn't a player in existence who doesn't sooner or later recall his triumphs. Who can resist the indulgence of lingering on a beautiful moment? I know I can't. To tell you the truth, I love these hands and looked forward to the nocturnal pleasure of soaking in their warmth. But it's hard to play well when you're tired, and so sometimes when you're really exhausted, the only way to get a good night's sleep is to take a sleeping pill.

But even that isn't always enough. I remember one evening near the end of the second round-robin. We had two or three matches to play and, needing a good rest, I had gone to bed early. About two in the morning I was awakened by an insistent knocking on the door. When I realized it wouldn't go away, I opened my door to find a smiling if tipsy blonde with two glasses of brandy clutched precariously in her hands. I recognized her from one of the cocktail parties earlier in the tournament. Without waiting for an invitation, she declared her intention of coming in to finish her drink(s).

It was quite possible that she had been sent to me by one of the opposing teams to prevent me resting, so that I wouldn't play well the following day. On the other hand, if she had genuinely come seeking hospitality, it was my duty to show her some. I could have been selfish and gone back to sleep, or I could have sacrificed myself and shown her the traditional hospitality associated with the East.

Always a patriot, I won't tell you which path I chose – I will only tell you that kindness and decency have their own reward. The next day I played with added vigour, and we easily won both our matches. If the whole thing had been a Machiavellian plot by one of our opponents to spike me, it didn't work.

When the round-robin stage finished, we found that we had not only qualified but were lying second to America. This was beyond our wildest expectations. It was embarrassing only to Fazli, who was so sure we would be knocked out at this stage, that he had booked his return flight for the next day. He had to buy a new ticket!

In the semifinal, we played against Argentina, the South American champions, while the United States played Poland. With luck comes confidence, and when the semifinal started, our whole team was still playing on Heat 1, feeling unstoppable. My partner, Masood, is usually an intense and emotionless player, but even he found a smile when the opponents bid a grand slam where he was looking at the ace of trumps.

This was the hand:

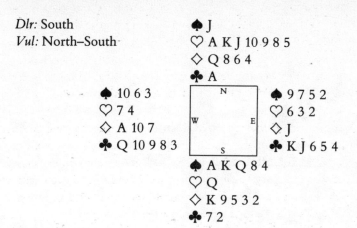

Dlr: South
Vul: North–South

North:
♠ J
♡ A K J 10 9 8 5
♢ Q 8 6 4
♣ A

West:
♠ 10 6 3
♡ 7 4
♢ A 10 7
♣ Q 10 9 8 3

East:
♠ 9 7 5 2
♡ 6 3 2
♢ J
♣ K J 6 5 4

South:
♠ A K Q 8 4
♡ Q
♢ K 9 5 3 2
♣ 7 2

Open Room:

West	North	East	South
Masood		Zia	
			1 ♠
Pass	2 ♡	Pass	3 ♢
Pass	4 ♣	Dble	4 ♢
Pass	5 ♣	Pass	5 ♢
Pass	6 ♢	Pass	Pass
7 ♣	Pass	Pass	7 ♢
Dble	Pass	Pass	Pass

Closed Room:

West	North	East	South
	Nishat		Nisar
			1 ♠
Pass	3 ♡	Pass	4 ♢
Pass	5 ♢	Pass	Pass
Pass			

If Masood hadn't sacrificed in seven clubs, it isn't clear what would have happened in six diamonds. In the other room, Nisar guessed the trumps correctly to win twelve tricks for plus 620. In our room, South guessed them too, but he was in seven doubled. One down doubled gave us 200 and thirteen imps.

One of my rubber-bridge tips came through at the right moment, on board nine of the semifinal.

Dlr: North
Vul: East–West

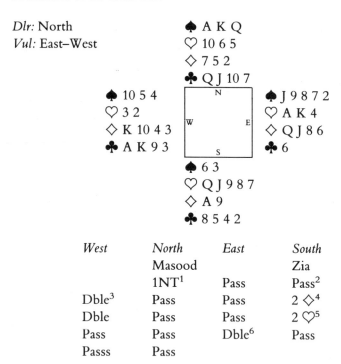

```
                    ♠ A K Q
                    ♡ 10 6 5
                    ◇ 7 5 2
                    ♣ Q J 10 7
    ♠ 10 5 4           N        ♠ J 9 8 7 2
    ♡ 3 2                       ♡ A K 4
    ◇ K 10 4 3    W       E     ◇ Q J 8 6
    ♣ A K 9 3          S        ♣ 6
                    ♠ 6 3
                    ♡ Q J 9 8 7
                    ◇ A 9
                    ♣ 8 5 4 2
```

West	North	East	South
	Masood		Zia
	1NT[1]	Pass	Pass[2]
Dble[3]	Pass	Pass	2 ◇[4]
Dble	Pass	Pass	2 ♡[5]
Pass	Pass	Dble[6]	Pass
Passs	Pass		

[1] 12–14 points.
[2] It's usually better to pass a weak notrump rather than to take out to two hearts when you cannot handle a two-spade bid by the opponents.
[3] Frisky, to say the least.
[4] I wanted to be doubled in two hearts, so I set the bait.
[5] Closing in for the kill.
[6] Hooked.

I had no trouble making two hearts doubled for plus 470.

These two hands were typical of the way things were going for us. We were sailing along – but suddenly there was a hiccup, or two hiccups to be exact.

The World Bridge Federation had recently started using 'screens' for major events. The 'screen' consists of a board with a small curtain in it placed diagonally across the table so that partners cannot see each other. Your bids are made by placing pieces of cardboard in a tray, which slides under the curtain during the auction. The purpose is to remove any accidental or intentional voice inflections. After the bidding, the curtain is raised so that the players can see the cards, but not one another's faces. The board runs under the table as well so that partners' feet may not touch.

Instances of cheating at the top level are few and far between, but when they do occur, they receive vast amounts of publicity which is detrimental to the game. So the authorities try to ensure security in tournaments as best they can. Most of the top players prefer screens – I for one love not always having to control my reactions, which I must do when there are no screens around. By nature I am very demonstrative and emotional. I like the freedom of smiling or even grimacing at my partner while he is playing or bidding a hand. This is fine only if he can't see me, which is the case behind screens.

Not being able to hear or see your partner make his bid, as you've been used to all your life, can sometimes be confusing. With little experience at this level or practice with screens, it was not surprising that we had an accident or two. On two separate occasions one of our players mis-saw the bidding and ended up at a high level in the opponents' suit – going for big numbers.

But this was the only small problem we had, and we ended up winning the semifinal in some comfort America winning the other.

Fazli had never wanted to play. Before one session, the Chief Tournament Director came up and said that he was lying on the ground, holding his leg and groaning. I went with the CTD to see him. One glance told me that this was a sham. I asked the director to leave me alone with Fazli. 'Fazli, we have called a doctor,' I told him, 'but he says that his basic fee is $500, which you will have to pay before he will look at you.' Fazli was up and ready in less time than it took me to type that!

We were in the final of the world championship! Where were those who said we shouldn't be? Where were those who said Pakistan could only play physical sports like cricket, squash and hockey?

By now we were the Cinderella team, and the whole world loves an underdog. All the spectators were rooting for us. We were over the moon.

It was hard for us to buckle down to playing well in the final. We had already surpassed our own expectations. The Americans on the other hand had come expecting to reach this stage: They were mentally prepared for this moment; for them the battle was just starting.

Our best chance, perhaps our only chance, would be if we could score enough points to take a large lead while the American sponsor was playing. American teams are often made up of five full-time professionals and one sponsor who hires them. The sponsor is an enthusiast whose standard is usually below international level. To be called a World Champion though, each player had to play at least one-third of the deals.

Our free-style and aggressive game was very effective in scoring heavily from weaker players, just as it could be inferior when faced with the methods of better players. We had been hoping that while the sponsor played his third of the match, we would have our one chance of really doing well. But an unexpected blow was waiting for us. For the first time in such a situation, the American team decided it was too dangerous to play their own sponsor against us, and, with his agreement, they decided to sit him out for the whole final. The merits or demerits of this action were not our business. We did know that it was a severe blow to our hopes of victory.

The final was over 96 boards, and after 48 the score was: Pakistan 95 USA 92. It was halfway though the final and we were leading. Did we really have a chance? Sadly, now the tide turned and as the miracle slipped away, we came quickly back to earth.

There are always regrets. There were many hands on which we could have played better. Masood and I were especially tired, having played almost six hundred deals without a rest. But the hand that generated the most publicity was certainly this one:

Sitting West with neither side vulnerable, you pick up this hand:

♠ Q 9 8 7 ♡ A Q 9 6 4 ◇ 6 ♣ K 9 7

The auction proceeds as follows:

West	North	East	South
1 ♡	3 ♡[1]	Dble	3NT[2]
Pass	Pass	Dble[3]	Pass
Pass	Redble[4]	Pass	Pass
Pass			

[1] 'Partner, I have a solid (minor) suit on the side; please bid three notrumps if you have a heart stopper.'
[2] 'I have a heart stopper.'
[3] 'I don't think they can make this.'
[4] 'I am worried about the whole affair. I have my solid suit, but nothing else.'

As you think about your lead, I should tell you that your opponents are the famous pair, Jeff Meckstroth and Eric Rodwell, who, as usual, are involved in a potentially huge swing. Take your time, the Americans are up 68 imps and the fate of the World Championship may hinge on your lead. What is your choice?

Leading a heart is *bad* because North–South probably have seven diamond tricks, the king of hearts and one black ace. In fact, on a heart lead, declarer would have made ten tricks for plus 950 and thirteen imps.

If you selected a spade, you would have been minus 750 and twelve imps.

Finally, if you picked a club, you would have been plus 2200 and twenty imps! The defenders can win the first *ten* tricks!

Our player judged to lead a spade.

This was the full deal:

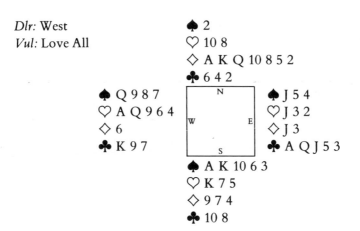

Dlr: West
Vul: Love All

North:
♠ 2
♡ 10 8
◇ A K Q 10 8 5 2
♣ 6 4 2

West:
♠ Q 9 8 7
♡ A Q 9 6 4
◇ 6
♣ K 9 7

East:
♠ J 5 4
♡ J 3 2
◇ J 3
♣ A Q J 5 3

South:
♠ A K 10 6 3
♡ K 7 5
◇ 9 7 4
♣ 10 8

I could give you many arguments for and against the various leads, but I prefer not to talk about this hand any longer than necessary – it still hurts too much.

As the points slipped away steadily, and the dream with them, we didn't give up. But fighting from behind is not easy, and this often made matters even worse. However, there were some cheeky moments.

This was board 67:

Dlr: South
Vul: E–W

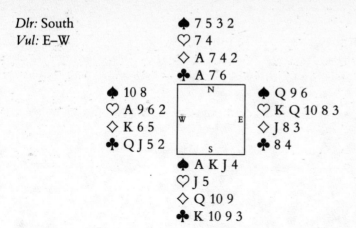

```
                      ♠ 7 5 3 2
                      ♡ 7 4
                      ◇ A 7 4 2
                      ♣ A 7 6
        ♠ 10 8            N        ♠ Q 9 6
        ♡ A 9 6 2                 ♡ K Q 10 8 3
        ◇ K 6 5     W        E    ◇ J 8 3
        ♣ Q J 5 2                 ♣ 8 4
                         S
                      ♠ A K J 4
                      ♡ J 5
                      ◇ Q 10 9
                      ♣ K 10 9 3
```

I was in one notrump – yes, I know two spades is a better contract, but that's one of the problems of playing weak notrumps. I received the two-of-clubs lead: six, eight, ten. I returned the three of clubs, West put in the jack, and I won with dummy's ace.

Now I called for the four of hearts: three, jack, two! Yes, a heart to the jack held!

This deceptive play often works, even against the best opposition, as you see here. It looks flamboyant, but requires no great level of ability. Whenever you're in a notrump contract and can see the defenders are about to switch to a suit you can't stand, try the effect of playing the suit *before* they do – it might mislead them. It is much better than giving up.

Sometimes this play can lead to unexpected benefits. Here is an example of Gabriel Chagas, the Brazilian star in action.

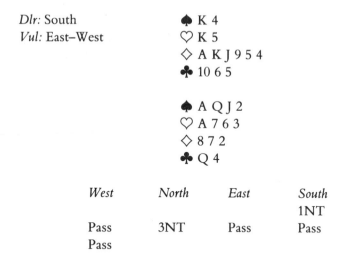

Dlr: South
Vul: East–West

♠ K 4
♡ K 5
♢ A K J 9 5 4
♣ 10 6 5

♠ A Q J 2
♡ A 7 6 3
♢ 8 7 2
♣ Q 4

West	North	East	South
			1NT
Pass	3NT	Pass	Pass
Pass			

There was no problem. West led the six of spades. Happy to have avoided a club lead, Chagas counted his top tricks and found eight: four spades, two hearts and two diamonds. If the diamonds were coming in, if they were good, he didn't need four spade tricks. So he won the first trick with dummy's king of spades and dropped the jack from hand as a 'just in case' play. I wasn't sure quite why; it just seemed like a good idea at the time.

However, when he cashed the ace of diamonds, West discarded the three of spades.

If ever a contract looked hopeless, this was it. He invoked Rule Number One: In such situations, play their suit before they do. Chagas I called for the five of clubs and put up the queen. West won with the ace, and didn't sneeringly shoot back a club. Instead he switched to a heart.

Thanks to the play on the first trick, no longer did Chagas even have the eight tricks he started with. But, hoping to induce a second spade discard from West, he led another diamond. West obliged by discarding a spade, giving the spade trick back. It was a lot of work to break even.

Not willing yet to give up by cashing his eight tricks and thinking that it was worth the investment to risk going two down, Chagas ducked the diamond to East's ten.

He was still alive when East returned a heart to the ace. This was the end-position:

♠ 4
♡ —
◇ K J 5 4
♣ 10 6

♠ A Q 2
♡ 7 6
◇ 8
♣ 4

Chagas cashed his three spade tricks, West throwing a heart on the third, and East, in obvious discomfort, pitching the eight and jack of clubs. Now he exited with a heart. West won, then led a club to East's bare king. He was endplayed, forced to lead into dummy's king-jack of diamonds.

Chagas +600, Brazilian magic at its best. This was the full hand:

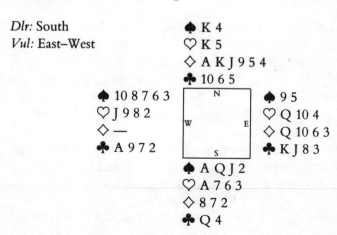

Dlr: South
Vul: East–West

♠ K 4
♡ K 5
◇ A K J 9 5 4
♣ 10 6 5

♠ 10 8 7 6 3
♡ J 9 8 2
◇ —
♣ A 9 7 2

♠ 9 5
♡ Q 10 4
◇ Q 10 6 3
♣ K J 8 3

♠ A Q J 2
♡ A 7 6 3
◇ 8 7 2
♣ Q 4

Even the best players can be fooled by this bold deceptive play. If you twisted my arm, I could probably recall a hand recorded live for British television a few years ago when Rob Sheehan, the English international, made almost the identical play against me. Rather embarrassingly, I ducked much to the amusement of a couple of million views.

As time ran out in Rye we did have a few defiant moments. Masood had played to the point of exhaustion, and now, beaten but not bowed, his hand, board 92, was a fitting tribute to his efforts:

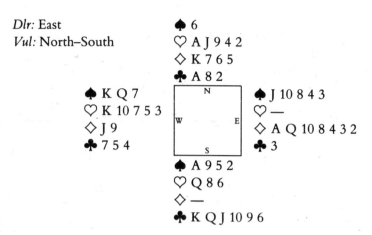

Dlr: East
Vul: North–South

```
                    ♠ 6
                    ♡ A J 9 4 2
                    ◇ K 7 6 5
                    ♣ A 8 2
  ♠ K Q 7                          ♠ J 10 8 4 3
  ♡ K 10 7 5 3         N           ♡ —
  ◇ J 9          W          E       ◇ A Q 10 8 4 3 2
  ♣ 7 5 4                          ♣ 3
                    S
                    ♠ A 9 5 2
                    ♡ Q 8 6
                    ◇ —
                    ♣ K Q J 10 9 6
```

This was what happened in the Closed Room:

West	North	East	South
Nisar	Arnold	Nishat	Levin
			1 ♣
1 ♡	2 ◇	Pass	2 ♠
Pass	2NT	Pass	3 ♣
Pass	3NT	Pass	Pass
Pass			

Nishat led the three of spades: ace, king, six. Declarer led the queen of hearts, covered by the king and ace. Now with the marked finesse of the nine of hearts, Arnold had ten top tricks.

The action in the Open Room was more exciting.

West	North	East	South
Rodwell	Zia	Meckstroth	Masood
		1 ♢	Dble
1 ♡	Dble	1 ♠	2 ♣
2 ♠	4NT	5 ♡	Pass[1]
5 ♠	Pass	Pass	6 ♣
Dble[2]	Pass	Pass	Redble
Pass	Pass	Pass	

[1] Systematically showing one ace.
[2] Knowing his partner is ruffing hearts

Meckstroth and Rodwell play Precision, but the one-diamond opening bid was light even by their standards. Rodwell's one-heart bid was natural and forcing for one round; and my double was for penalties.

By the time Rodwell bid two spades, I knew what was happening and tried to clarify matters for Masood by using Blackwood.

Now Meckstroth – bidding for a third time on his seven points! – made an expert call, pinpointing the lead.

Finally, Masood did brilliantly, bidding six clubs and redoubling. They might have been about to win the Bermuda Bowl, but he made sure they remembered we were there.

The play was short. The three-of-hearts lead (an upside-down suit-preference lead for spades!) was ruffed by East, and back came the jack of spades, won with the ace. Masood cashed the king of clubs, then led the queen of hearts, covered by the king and ace. He drew trumps, finessed the nine of hearts, and had twelve tricks by way of one spade, three hearts, two spade ruffs in the dummy and six trumps in hand. We scored +1780 and fifteen imps.

Despite losing the final we were not unhappy. The better team had won, which is as it should be, and we had vindicated our place in the tournament. Our players had done us proud, each one had played his heart out, and we could go home proudly with our silver medals. We hardly noticed that the medals proved to be more symbolic than real, being wooden cigarette boxes! Most of the team gave theirs to our delighted supporter, Beroze, who was crying with joy.

Among the lessons I learnt from the invaluable experience of this tournament were the following:

1 Team spirit is as important as ability. There were at least two teams that lost bushels of points because of the unfriendly attitudes of their members. Our strengths were friendship and camaraderie.

2 Never discuss a hand at the table – never.

3 There are a very few people who can have a disaster and suffer no adverse reaction, so whenever you have a disaster on a hand, regroup. By that I mean make a conscious effort to come to the next hand with a fresh mind. It is easy to be so caught up in a disaster without realizing that it affects you for several ensuing deals. If it helps, get up and drink a glass of iced water, or go to the washroom, or walk around the room. Do anything, but snap out of it or you're dead.

4 Partners and teams should meet daily after the game to go over all the hands of interest, especially those where partnerships had a problem. Everybody does have accidents; it's no big deal, but it is vital to clear the air and get out negative feelings from your system, rather than holding them in, feeling hurt or bitter. If at these sessions you feel your partner, yourself or a team-mate went crazy, say so. I recommend an open discussion so that it becomes less personal and more fun.

   We all commit idiocies from time to time – if you can accept that and laugh at them, you are heading in the right direction.

5 Understand the theory of the 3 Heats and *apply it*.

6 Bridge is unlike any other game. No team is so much better that the underdog doesn't have a chance.

7 Never give up, and remember above all that the real tournament only begins at the final, no matter how much it seems you have achieved before.

11

New York, New York

The 1980s and 1990s

On the way back from Rye, I stopped in New York. Everything you hear about the city is true – you either love it or hate it.

The first night I was there, a taxi-driver told me that I looked like a waiter for wearing a dinner jacket, and a 60-year-old woman in the hotel bar offered to take me dancing at Regines discotheque. The second night I was there, the 60-year-old woman told me that I looked like a waiter, and the taxi driver offered to take me dancing!

By the third night, I'd had enough. I stayed home and left the two of them to go out together. My kind of town. I loved it instantly.

New York is where the action is. First there is rubber bridge at the Cavendish Club, the Regency and the Mayfair; where the stakes range from low to astronomical, and where the players range from unbelievably bad to unbelievably good. Next there are the high-stake imp games (duplicate bridge) at the Mayfair and Cavendish. You draw for partners and team-mates, and play eight-board matches. They are great fun, and great practice too.

American and British bridge clubs are quite different. In New York rubber-bridge games, you can play as many systems as you like. In Britain, some say that even Stayman and Blackwood should be banned. Reactions to errors have slightly different flavours too. In New York, you are more likely to hear someone called by the endearing Americanism, 'You mother******!' than the more British reprimand, 'Nasty setback, partner.'

My first visit was to the Cavendish, famous for its annual auction tournament where the pairs are 'sold' to bidders. I naturally came to play, but on the first occasion I watched. Kibitzing can be boring, unless someone of the calibre of 'Broadway' Billy Eisenberg is playing the hand. I'm not easily impressed, but he managed it, Chinese style. Billy is the only person who has been World Champion at bridge and backgammon at the same time. He had the doubtful distinction of resigning from the famous Aces team. They didn't allow enough enough late nights in a week to suit him. He likes the fast lane.

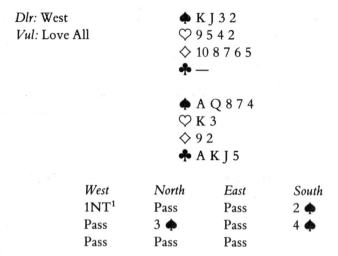

Dlr: West   ♠ K J 3 2
Vul: Love All   ♡ 9 5 4 2
                ◇ 10 8 7 6 5
                ♣ —

                ♠ A Q 8 7 4
                ♡ K 3
                ◇ 9 2
                ♣ A K J 5

West	North	East	South
1NT[1]	Pass	Pass	2 ♠
Pass	3 ♠	Pass	4 ♠
Pass	Pass	Pass	

[1] 15–17 points.

West leads the ten of spades. How would you play?

You have twenty-one points between you and dummy, giving East a maximum of four points. You work out that West must have the ace of hearts – as if East had it, West would have led a top diamond from his honours. There's obviously no genuine chance to make the hand – unless you try the 'Chinese' finesse. (A finesse that can never work if the opponents cover your card, i.e. a phoney finesse with A2 opposite Q3 if you run the nine it holds.) That's what Eisenberg did. He won the opening lead with the queen of spades, and at trick two ran the jack of clubs, throwing a heart from the dummy!

Then he discarded two more heart losers on the ace and king of clubs. This was the full deal:

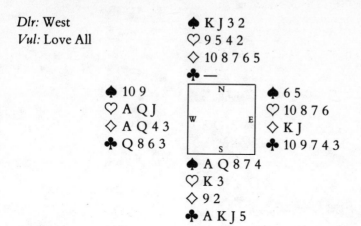

Dlr: West
Vul: Love All

♠ K J 3 2
♡ 9 5 4 2
♢ 10 8 7 6 5
♣ —

♠ 10 9
♡ A Q J
♢ A Q 4 3
♣ Q 8 6 3

♠ 6 5
♡ 10 8 7 6
♢ K J
♣ 10 9 7 4 3

♠ A Q 8 7 4
♡ K 3
♢ 9 2
♣ A K J 5

Would you have covered the jack of clubs?

The Chinese finesse works quite often. Officially it's a no-play play, but it comes up more often than you might imagine.

Desperate bidders need desperate plays:

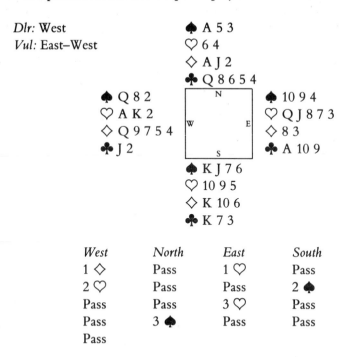

Dlr: West

Vul: East–West

```
              ♠ A 5 3
              ♡ 6 4
              ◇ A J 2
              ♣ Q 8 6 5 4
♠ Q 8 2             N          ♠ 10 9 4
♡ A K 2                        ♡ Q J 8 7 3
◇ Q 9 7 5 4   W         E      ◇ 8 3
♣ J 2                          ♣ A 10 9
                    S
              ♠ K J 7 6
              ♡ 10 9 5
              ◇ K 10 6
              ♣ K 7 3
```

West	North	East	South
1 ◇	Pass	1 ♡	Pass
2 ♡	Pass	Pass	2 ♠
Pass	Pass	3 ♡	Pass
Pass	3 ♣	Pass	Pass
Pass			

True, you pushed them one too high, but your partner couldn't leave well alone. However, maybe you can even make three spades. West leads the ace of hearts: four, queen, five. He cashes the king of hearts: six, three, ten, then switches to the jack of clubs: four, ten, king. How do you continue?

With two hearts already lost and two clubs still to lose, you need to make four spade tricks. For a start, they must break 3–3. But from his opening bid and the play so far, West is marked with the queen. The only chance is to play as if you have the ten of spades. Lead the jack from hand and hope he doesn't cover.

If West doesn't cover, ruff your heart loser in the dummy, cash the ace of spades, play a diamond to the king, draw trumps and take the diamond finesse.

I had intended to stay in New York one week. I was still there a month later. During my visit, I could soon see that the top Americans had thought deeply about parts of the game that hadn't even been considered by most of the world.

Take this hand: You, West, hold:

♠ A 7 4 3 ♡ A 7 4 3 ◇ 10 8 2 ♣ 7 6

The bidding is short: South opens five clubs and everybody passes.

You've read your text-books and lead the ace of spades. After the dummy is tabled, this is what you can see:

Dlr: South

Vul: East–West

<pre>
                    ♠ Q 6 5
                    ♡ Q 6 5
                    ◇ A K Q J 5
                    ♣ 8 2
        ♠ A 7 4 3
        ♡ A 7 4 3
        ◇ 10 8 2
        ♣ 7 6
</pre>

On your ace of spades, partner plays an encouraging eight of spades. You're a careful player and cash the ace of hearts. Partner plays the nine of hearts. Well, well, he's got both kings. Which one do you cash?

If you gave this problem to 99 per cent of the world, they would all reply with learned and doubtful logic. The truth is that they wouldn't have a clue. If you had ever met 'The Beast', it would be easy. The Beast – alias Ira Rubin – has a simple rule: In cash-out situations, a high odd card shows encouragement with an odd number in the suit, and a high even card shows an original even number. Simple yet effective. So in the above example the eight of spades would have shown four spades, and the nine of hearts, five hearts. You would cash your partner's king of spades.

The full hand was:

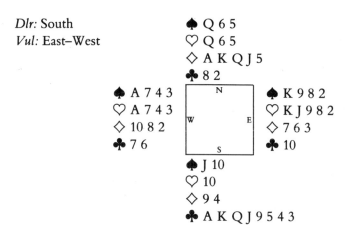

Dlr: South
Vul: East–West

North: ♠ Q 6 5 / ♡ Q 6 5 / ♢ A K Q J 5 / ♣ 8 2

West: ♠ A 7 4 3 / ♡ A 7 4 3 / ♢ 10 8 2 / ♣ 7 6

East: ♠ K 9 8 2 / ♡ K J 9 8 2 / ♢ 7 6 3 / ♣ 10

South: ♠ J 10 / ♡ 10 / ♢ 9 4 / ♣ A K Q J 9 5 4 3

The same principle can apply when you've overcalled in a suit. Partner leads a high card, say the ace or king, you can signal encouragement as well as give the count at the same time. If partner doesn't have the appropriate odd or even card, you won't be worse off than you were before.

Rubin was one of the regular regulars at the Cavendish. He was nicknamed The Beast for his monstrous behaviour and his attacks, physical as well as verbal, on everybody – partners and opponents alike. He is 6′4″ tall and gargles razor-blades for breakfast. He has lived up to his reputation many times.

I remember an incident when he was playing with Matt Granovetter. Matt forgot to win a trick, letting a contract that should have been easy to beat through. Anticipating Rubin's wrath, he ran to the men's bathroom, hoping to find shelter in a well-bolted cubicle. Nothing is safe from The Beast. Rubin not only followed him there, he even climbed over the wall in an insane rage to continue his attack on him at closer quarters.

Rubin is impossible to play with or against; but like so many of the inhabitants of the bridge world, he veers between genius and monster. I've learnt a lot from him as in his more 'human' moments; he is an encyclopædia of useful bridge information.

First, there was this hand. You're West:

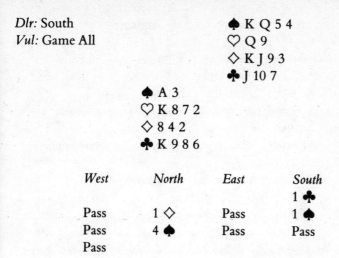

Dlr: South
Vul: Game All

```
                        ♠ K Q 5 4
                        ♡ Q 9
                        ◇ K J 9 3
                        ♣ J 10 7
        ♠ A 3
        ♡ K 8 7 2
        ◇ 8 4 2
        ♣ K 9 8 6
```

West	North	East	South
			1 ♣
Pass	1 ◇	Pass	1 ♠
Pass	4 ♠	Pass	Pass
Pass			

You open with the ace of spades. What do you lead at trick two?

Most people would answer, 'It's a guess.'

Rubin proposed an easy solution: suit preference in the trump suit. On this hand partner would play the jack of spades under the ace, asking for a heart switch.

The full deal:

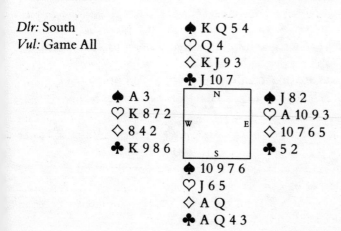

Dlr: South
Vul: Game All

```
                        ♠ K Q 5 4
                        ♡ Q 4
                        ◇ K J 9 3
                        ♣ J 10 7
        ♠ A 3            N           ♠ J 8 2
        ♡ K 8 7 2                    ♡ A 10 9 3
        ◇ 8 4 2     W       E        ◇ 10 7 6 5
        ♣ K 9 8 6                    ♣ 5 2
                        S
                        ♠ 10 9 7 6
                        ♡ J 6 5
                        ◇ A Q
                        ♣ A Q 4 3
```

By the time I was ready to leave New York, two things were clear: there were more good players in America than anywhere else. If I wanted to compete with the best, I had to start spending time there.

So I added the States to my growing list of homes. I hopped from one country to another, running through passports like packs of cards. It was a strange feeling when someone asked me, 'Where do you live?' I had to reply, 'I don't know.' But that was the truth.

Although it may sound so, the travelling wasn't glamorous. I was motivated neither by the lure of making money (most tournaments are strictly amateur) nor by the celebrity status of a bridge player (there isn't any).

Cricketers and footballers might need bodyguards to keep girls out of their rooms; bridge plyers usually hire them to bring them in. As for the 'celebrity' idea – to the public, even the better-known bridge players are usually no more than names in a newspaper column. I remember visiting a club in the Middle East where, before I could introduce myself, one of the players asked me if I knew his good friend Zia Mahmood!

On the other hand, to find something that you really enjoy is a bonus not to be taken lightly. Moreover, while most people dream about retiring and wandering around the world to follow their passions, I was already doing just that. As George Raft once said: 'Part of my money went on gambling, part went on horses, part went on women – and the rest I spent foolishly.'

And I have loved every moment.

Wall Street is packed with good bridge players. None better known than Alan 'Ace' Greenberg and Jimmy Cayne, Chairman and President of Bear Sterns. On one visit to New York, I happened to join their team for the prestigious Reisinger tournament. We ended up winning. That was good news. A lucky hand turned out to be even better news.

Sitting West, you hold:

♠ 9 7 4 3 ♡ 6 2 ◇ 5 4 ♣ Q 10 8 4 2

And hear the following:

West	North	East	South
			1 ♣
Pass	1 ♡	Pass	1NT[1]
Pass	3 ♡[2]	Pass	3NT
Pass	Pass	Pass	

[1] Showing 15–17 points.
[2] Forcing.

What is your lead?

Have a look at the whole hand before deciding:

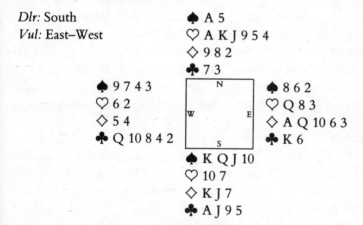

Dlr: South
Vul: East–West

♠ A 5
♡ A K J 9 5 4
◇ 9 8 2
♣ 7 3

♠ 9 7 4 3
♡ 6 2
◇ 5 4
♣ Q 10 8 4 2

♠ 8 6 2
♡ Q 8 3
◇ A Q 10 6 3
♣ K 6

♠ K Q J 10
♡ 10 7
◇ K J 7
♣ A J 9 5

The contract looks impregnable. Instead of the conventional standard lead such as fourth best in spades, I led the *four* of diamonds! Look what happened. My partner, Matt Granovetter, liked the lead. Playing his part, he won with the ace and returned the three, in theory showing that he had started with four diamonds.

The declarer was worried that if he finessed the jack of diamonds, I might win with the queen and switch to a club. So, he rightly won with the king of diamonds. After all, he was safe on any distribution except East's having five diamonds, which was 'impossible' on the play.

Declarer took the heart finesse – and almost fell off his chair when Matt won with the queen of hearts and cashed *three* diamond tricks.

Why this 'strange' lead? First, I have a theory that it's correct to try something unusual in a desperate situation. This hand fitted nicely: our prospects looked hopeless. Second, South was known to have at least four clubs as he denied three hearts when he bid three notrumps. So a club lead was out; anyway, I hate leading the opponents' suits. Third, partner couldn't have good spades because he didn't overcall one spade. And fourth, he may hold good diamonds without the values for a two-level intervention. The 'normal' lead is the five, but with such a terrible hand, I thought I might as well try the effect of a false-card: the four. Who knows, maybe something good would happen.

It did. The declarer went down; and Ace and Jimmy enjoyed the lead so much that they invited me into the most exclusive club in the world, the Regency Whist Club on East 67th and 5th Avenue.

The Regency

'Rockefeller hasn't got any money.'

'What do you mean, he's worth over $50 million.'

'That's just what I mean, he hasn't got any money.'

If you had happened to overhear that conversation in one of the plush rooms of the Regency Whist Club, you wouldn't have been too surprised. There are people who have money, and there are people who are rich.

Most bridge games have a few interesting people, this one had nothing but. With regulars like the Nose, the Fox and the Weasel, you might mistakenly think that you were dealing with a strange group. In fact the game boasted some of the most powerful men in America – and some of the most generous.

Take Milton.

Milton Petrie is in his late eighties. He loves bridge with a passion, plays daily and is always the first to arrive at the club. Well known for his wealth, he is even better known for his philanthrophy. When he is cut out of the rubber, he scours newspapers, picking out deserving cases to give a helping hand to. A real-life Father Christmas, he hands out money to worthwhile causes as if it's going out of style. Most of his donations are made anonymously, but I heard about one six-figure contribution that he made to an orphanage. When the grateful beneficiaries turned up at his office to thank him, Petrie doubled the donation.

If a policeman or fireman is killed in the line of duty, his family could well have a trust fund set up to help them – courtesy of Petrie. He enjoys his daily 'fix' of bridge, but avoids unnecessary conversation. In fact I had been playing at the club for two days before he said a word to me. Then I almost wished it hadn't stayed that way. This was the diamond suit. The contract was three notrumps, and dummy had no side entry.

Dummy
$\diamond$ A Q J 9 3

Partner   *Zia*
$\diamond$ 8 7 5 4 $\diamond$ K 2

Petrie
$\diamond$ 10 6

When Petrie ran the ten, I ducked my king. When he didn't guess what I had done, he finessed again, going down when he would have made the contract if I had won the first diamond trick.

When he saw what I had done, he first growled, 'You son of a bitch.' Then he smiled and added, 'Nice play.'

Jack Dreyfus, founder of the Dreyfus Mutual Fund, is another committed bridge lover. Successful in everything he's tried: golf, tennis, even gin-rummy, he's also had his share of luck. Years ago he was confident that 3-D pictures would be the thing of the future. He put most of his money into Polaroid shares. 3-D was a disaster, but the company invented a new camera. The stock soared and Dreyfus used his 3-D glasses to count the fortune he made. Now retired, Dreyfus has diverted his time and wealth to his charitable medical foundation. He's also famous for somehow always dealing himself the ace of spades, but he may well make the Guinness Book of Records for having put down the best dummy in history – this one:

$\spadesuit$ A $\heartsuit$ A K J 10 9 8 7 6 3 2 $\diamond$ A $\clubsuit$ 4

The story is easier to understand if you hear that his partner was the lovable but, on occasion, disaster-prone 'Fox'.

Dreyfus dealt and opened two clubs.

The Fox bid the negative two diamonds.

Dreyfus' RHO leapt to five clubs.

Dreyfus 'closed' the auction with a bid of six hearts.

Well, almost closed.

He hadn't got past the Fox, who still had to show his $\spadesuit$ Q J 9 8 7 6 3.

'Six spades!' he offered.

Dreyfus gave up. Seven hearts had no chance, and who knew what spades the Fox held. Not enough.

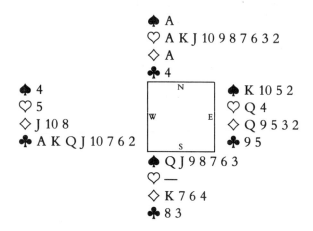

♠ A
♡ A K J 10 9 8 7 6 3 2
♢ A
♣ 4

♠ 4
♡ 5
♢ J 10 8
♣ A K Q J 10 7 6 2

♠ K 10 5 2
♡ Q 4
♢ Q 9 5 3 2
♣ 9 5

♠ Q J 9 8 7 6 3
♡ —
♢ K 7 6 4
♣ 8 3

One of the calmest people in the world, Dreyfus didn't say a word as the Fox went three down. But it was when the Fox said, 'Couldn't you rebid your hearts once?' that he exploded.

You can't stay mad at the Fox for long. He has a habit of coming up with one of his original remarks that is sure to make you laugh. Once when he had seemed totally unsurprised that our hopeless contract had made, I asked him if he realized how lucky we had been. 'Oh yes, of course I know. But I'm Jewish, miracles are quite common in our religion.' What else could a simple Pakistani say but, 'Oi vay!'

Sam Stayman is another regular at the Regency. His name must be the best known in the whole bridge world. Already in his eighties, he still plays as well as he did when winning his three world titles in the fifties.

Alan Sontag, in his book, *The Bridge Bum*, relates a story about someone who was invited to Stayman's Park Avenue apartment.

Almost immediately, the visitor gasped, 'This must cost you a fortune.' 'No,' replied Stayman, 'it costs me nothing. I own the whole block.' Stayman played this hand in New York in 1949.

Dlr: South
Vul: Game All

Dummy
♠ A 7
♡ Q 8 4
♢ A Q 2
♣ A Q 10 9 3

Declarer
♠ K Q 5
♡ A K 10 2
♢ K 10 4
♣ K 6 4

West	North	East	South
			1NT
Pass	4 ♣[1]	Pass	4 ♡[2]
Pass	5 ♣[3]	Pass	5 ♢[4]
Pass	7NT	Pass	Pass
Pass			

[1] Gerber, asking for aces.
[2] Showing one ace.
[3] Gerber, asking for kings.
[4] Four kings.

West led the jack of spades. What is your line of play?

It looks too easy – which is when an expert becomes doubly careful. Stayman seemed to have fourteen top tricks: three spades, three hearts, three diamonds and five clubs. The only problem would arise if the clubs broke badly. The real expert postpones the moment of truth.

Stayman cashed the ace of clubs, just to check they weren't 5–0, then took his major-suit winners, discarding a club from the dummy on the third spade. East pitched low diamonds on both the third spade and third heart. Finally, Stayman cashed the king of diamonds and led a diamond to the ace, everyone following.

He paused to count. West was known to have started with six spades, four hearts, two diamonds and one club. East had to have begun with four clubs. Stayman called for the ten of clubs and ran it. He led a club to the king, a diamond to the queen, and cashed the queen of clubs for his contract.

You are never too young or too old to start playing duplicate. Last year Petrie and Dreyfus took the plunge when they joined a team representing Corporate America. They played a match against the British Parliamentary team. Their team was impressive. Captained by Larry Tisch, Chairman of CBS Television, it included names whose very mention could affect the Dow Jones index: Jimmy Cayne, Ace Greenberg, Milton Petrie, George Gillespie III, Warren Buffett and Malcolm Forbes. No less impressive were their opponents: the Duke of Atholl, Lord Lever and several MPs. They were captained by Sir Peter Emery. Also playing was Lord Smith, a famous surgeon who is equally famous in the bridge world for once removing 34 gallstones from the English bridge player Maurice Harrison-Gray, with the statement, 'Enough for a small slam in notrumps.'

The match was held in Malcolm Forbes' Battersea home. I was lucky to be asked to act as an MC – lucky because it gave me an opportunity to see Forbes' house. What a house! A journey into a private world of treasures that outshone any museum. Every inch of the walls was smothered by his unique collection of Victorian art. The corridors were packed to overflowing with priceless antiques. Fabergé eggs were casually spread around like shells on a beach.

Forbes, who once openly declared that bridge was much more fascinating than making money, spent the day alternately charming the players and playing in the match. He certainly knew his way around the card table.

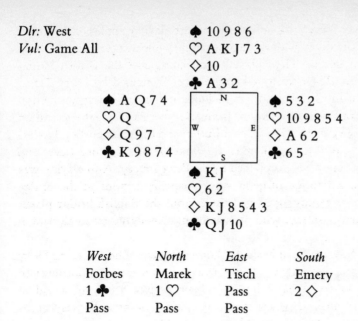

Dlr: West
Vul: Game All

	♠ 10 9 8 6
	♡ A K J 7 3
	◇ 10
	♣ A 3 2

♠ A Q 7 4   ♠ 5 3 2
♡ Q   ♡ 10 9 8 5 4
◇ Q 9 7   ◇ A 6 2
♣ K 9 8 7 4   ♣ 6 5

	♠ K J
	♡ 6 2
	◇ K J 8 5 4 3
	♣ Q J 10

West	North	East	South
Forbes	Marek	Tisch	Emery
1 ♣	1 ♡	Pass	2 ◇
Pass	Pass	Pass	

Forbes led his singleton heart. Emery won in the dummy, then ran the
ten of diamonds, losing to West's queen. Now Forbes made a tricky
play, switching to the *nine* of clubs. However, declarer wasn't fooled,
running it to his queen. Next came the king of diamonds to East's ace.
Tisch could have given his partner a heart ruff, but he could see that that
would be the effective end of the defence. Instead, he made the excellent
play of returning his second club, Forbes playing the king to lock
declarer in the dummy.

Now the defenders had to collect two spades, two diamonds, a heart
ruff and a club ruff for one down.

The American team narrowly lost the match; but the following day
they lost much more. After returning to his New Jersey home, Malcolm
Forbes, a man who had a life-long love affair with life, died of a heart
attack.

12

Luck be a Lady

Atlantic City, the Final Day

Walking into the playing area just before one o'clock, I noticed that it appeared larger than the previous day. This was because most of the tables had been removed, leaving only ten: all that was needed for the forty remaining players.

For the first time the atmosphere seemed charged, the smiles of yesterday looked less warm, and the competitors glanced warily at each other sizing up the opposition. With the field reduced, the enemy was now more visible, more real. There were no soft touches left. The next two days would be tough.

The spectators seemed to sense the tension too. There were more of them, and they spoke quietly, even solemnly. There were even a couple of newspaper reporters, something that is almost unheard of at a bridge event. I hoped I would give them a story. My first partner was already at the table.

'Everything natural, if you don't mind. I play no conventions.'

I was slightly surprised by this admission, but it was fine by me. We would only play one board together, so 99 per cent of the time systems would make no difference anyway. Conventions come up less than people realize.

But today was in the one per cent bracket. I picked up:

$$\spadesuit \ 10\ 7\ 6 \ \heartsuit \ 5 \ \diamondsuit \ A\ Q\ 10 \ \clubsuit \ Q\ J\ 10\ 9\ 8\ 5.$$

The auction went like this:

West	North	East	South
	Zia		Partner
			2 ♠[1]
Pass	3 ♣	Pass	3 ♡
Pass	3 ♠	Pass	4 ♠
Pass	6 ♠	Pass	Pass
Pass			

[1] Strong two-bid.

My choices over four spades were restricted because we weren't using Blackwood. I could pass, exceedingly cautious, or bid five spades, a slight underbid, or jump to six spades, a gross overbid. Naturally I chose the overbid – hell, it was the first board. West led the three of diamonds, and this was what my partner could see:

Dlr: South
Vul: Love All

♠ 10 7 6
♡ 5
♢ A Q 10
♣ Q J 10 9 8 5

♠ A K Q J 9
♡ K Q J 7 2
♢ 5 2
♣ K

How would you play the hand?

In the embarrassing position of having two aces out, it's right to finesse the ten of diamonds, hoping to get rid of the club loser.

My partner coolly finessed the *queen* of diamonds, then played a club to his king and West's ace. Luckily West continued with another diamond. Now my partner drew trumps in three rounds ending in the dummy, then discarded all five heart losers on my club winners. Plus 980!

This was the full deal:

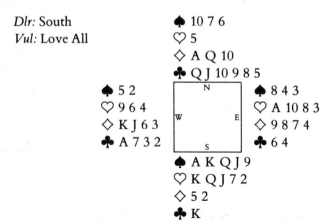

Dlr: South
Vul: Love All

```
                        ♠ 10 7 6
                        ♡ 5
                        ◇ A Q 10
                        ♣ Q J 10 9 8 5
         ♠ 5 2              N          ♠ 8 4 3
         ♡ 9 6 4                       ♡ A 10 8 3
         ◇ K J 6 3      W       E      ◇ 9 8 7 4
         ♣ A 7 3 2                     ♣ 6 4
                           S
                        ♠ A K Q J 9
                        ♡ K Q J 7 2
                        ◇ 5 2
                        ♣ K
```

A triumph for no conventions! When did a Blackwood player last bid and make a slam with two aces out? This was better than roulette.

Talking about two aces out, try this lead problem. You're West, holding:

♠ 4 ♡ A K J 10 6 5 ◇ 10 7 2 ♣ A Q 9

The auction proceeds along an unusual path:

West	North	East	South
			3 ♠
4 ♡	7 ♠	Pass	Pass
Pass			

Well, what is your lead?

After you decide, look at the whole hand.

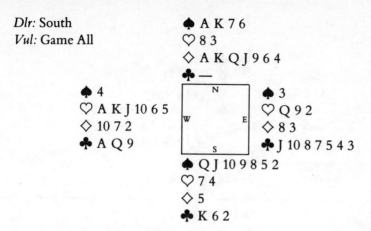

Dlr: South
Vul: Game All

```
                        ♠ A K 7 6
                        ♡ 8 3
                        ◇ A K Q J 9 6 4
                        ♣ —
        ♠ 4                              ♠ 3
        ♡ A K J 10 6 5                   ♡ Q 9 2
        ◇ 10 7 2                         ◇ 8 3
        ♣ A Q 9                          ♣ J 10 8 7 5 4 3
                        ♠ Q J 10 9 8 5 2
                        ♡ 7 4
                        ◇ 5
                        ♣ K 6 2
```

Nice bid, North! You didn't forget to ask who was sitting North, did you? Well, who it was doesn't matter as much as knowing what *type* of player it was. Against a tricky North, lead the ace or kings of hearts. Against a less tricky one, the ace of clubs is more likely to be right.

At the time, West led the ace of clubs. Minus 2210.

I don't mind admitting that at times I've been lucky in cards – sometime enormously so.

Some years ago, four of us were on board the *Canberra*, being filmed by the BBC for a TV series. We played Chicago-style rubber bridge for seven days for a nominal stake. At the end of the trip, the winner received a £10,000 prize.

As we entered the last deal of the final rubber, the Canadian, Sami Kehela, was leading, and I was second, 800 points behind. It didn't look good.

There were three passes to me, holding:

♠ A J 10 7   ♡ K 10 6   ◇ J 2   ♣ A K 10 9

I passed!

A Chicago stanza is only completed once all four hands are played. If a hand is passed out, it is redealt. Needing 800 points, I had to bid a slam or get an unlikely penalty. It was improbable that I could make a slam opposite a passed partner with only sixteen points. Maybe my next hand would be better.

Here I had already been lucky. Kehela, holding two aces, might have opened in the first seat. He knew I needed a slam to win, and that, holding two aces himself, I couldn't make one.

This was the new deal:

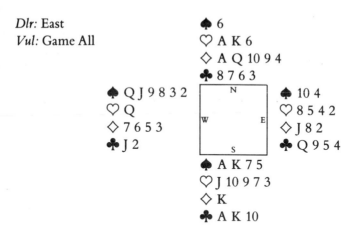

Dlr: East
Vul: Game All

♠ 6
♡ A K 6
♢ A Q 10 9 4
♣ 8 7 6 3

♠ Q J 9 8 3 2
♡ Q
♢ 7 6 5 3
♣ J 2

♠ 10 4
♡ 8 5 4 2
♢ J 8 2
♣ Q 9 5 4

♠ A K 7 5
♡ J 10 9 7 3
♢ K
♣ A K 10

West	North	East	South
Forrester	Zia	Kehela	Sundelin
		Pass	1 ♡
Pass	2 ♢	Pass	2 ♠
Pass	3 ♡	Pass	4 ♣
Pass	6 ♡	Pass	Pass
Pass			

My partner, P. O. Sundelin, a top Swedish international, and I bid and made six hearts for +1430. I had won the competition by six rubber-bridge points.

Yes, I have been lucky.

Good first boards are lucky for me, or maybe it's easier to play confidently with a good result behind you. Whatever the reasons, I felt things were going well. They were.

At the end of the session, I found I was sharing the lead with P. O. Sundelin. The pack was bunched close behind – but at least it was behind. They would have to wait until tomorrow.

Today Lady Luck belonged to me.

That Old Black Magic

Voodoo, witch doctors, spells and lucky potions – gamblers have running love affairs with Lady Luck, and bridge players will try anything once. To improve their fortune.

You're not like that? Wanna bet? When was the last time you said, 'Let's get out of these seats, they're unlucky.' Or, 'Give me the blues, the blues never lose.' Even fishing isn't sacred. Once I heard someone say, 'He's so lucky that if he put his backside in the river, he'd end up catching a fish.' (Although I'm not sure how lucky that would make him.)

These sayings go on and on. But how much of a part does luck really play in bridge? It's a tough question to answer. If we all lived for ever, probability states that everybody would have the same amount of luck. In the short run, some people are bound to be luckier than others.

Bridge players are always moaning about their bad luck. I've heard countless stories about losing streaks, but even the worst of them dries up sooner or later. And anyone is on a permanent losing run has more to worry about than just bad luck. Remember, the odds never lie, and a good player will always win in the long run, just like a casino.

Superstition – now that's another matter altogether. People who play cards are invariably superstitious. Some think clothes hold the answer. They say a lady is one who never shows her underwear unintentionally, but Nicola Gardener-Smith, an English women's world champion, has a preference for her lucky tartan underwear when she's playing in an important tournament – whatever turns you on.

Others stick to less personal items. Both Rixi Markus and Giorgio Belladonna are sure that pens have magical qualities. They keep switching them in synchronization with the ebb and flow of their sessions. They've won so much that maybe they know something.

Some think that transport is the answer. Brian Glubok, the American expert, believes that it's lucky to cycle to tournaments. Great – if you ever get there.

Others look to the heavens. A famous Italian player 'moons' to the moon every New Year's Eve. Asinine perhaps.

These and countless others are all possible, but I have my own way of escaping when things become desperate. Not long ago, a never-ending stream of losing confirmed my suspicions that the gods had finally deserted me. Things were so bad that there had even been times when I had actually thought of going back to work for a living. I badly needed a sign, a zinger, that would lift me up and put me back on the path of my winning ways of the past. I found one on Madison Avenue and 56th Street. A vision.

She hypnotized me and then she was gone. A voice, destiny, lady luck – who knows? – issued me with a challenge: 'Get her to have a drink with you and your run of luck will change.' What could I lose? I followed after her but she had disappeared. Frustrated, I got into the nearest cab. But luck was still playing her games, and as the cab started to move away from the curb, I spotted her again. She saw me, smiled and waved. It took me ten seconds to get over the shock, two seconds to yell, 'Stop!' to the cab driver and a throw a note at him, and about twenty seconds to run back along Madison Avenue to find her.

'I'm a gambler who's going through a terrible run of bad luck. I am extremely superstitious and I know that if you walk the ten blocks with me to my club, it's going to break the run that I've been having.'

Before she could reply, we started walking. If I was hypnotized before, now I was bewitched. Ten blocks later I had totally fallen for her.

'For the next three days I will go to the Mayfair Regent Hotel at six-thirty. I'll drink one glass of champagne and leave. If you'd like to see me again, come there. If not, it was a pleasure meeting you.'

What else could I say? She smiled, shook my hand and left. The next day, I nursed the champagne, but no one came. I was about to leave when a young man walked up to me.

'Are you Zia?' he asked. I nodded.

'My name is Luigi. I am a friend of Jacqueline's. She can't see you.' But he handed me an envelope.

'I'll be here tomorrow . . .' I started to say, but he was already on his way out. Who was she? Who was he? The whole thing was like a mystery. The envelope contained one of those cards that you buy in a shop – sweet words, but the message was clear: 'Goodbye'. That only made things worse. I couldn't get her out of my mind; she was becoming an obsession.

I was there the next day, sure that I would never see her again.

I was wrong. She was waiting . . .

. . . with Luigi!

But she had literally come to say goodbye – she was going away.

'Will you see me when you return?'

'Maybe.'

But maybe wasn't nearly enough. I told her that the matter was no longer in our hands – destiny had taken over. How else could she explain the way that we had met? I also complained about the impersonal, printed card, saying that I would have written something original.

'You're a gambler. Write me something yourself and if I like it, I'll have dinner with you when I come back.' Infatuation inspired eloquence and I wrote:

> I thought I saw a friendly wave,
> But when I looked again, it was a wand that
> waved its magic on my mind.
> I sat to look into the coolness of your eyes
> but saw instead the softness of your soul.
> I tried to touch your hand, but it was gone,
> already reaching out to steal my heart.
> And when you walked away, you didn't leave
> but stayed – a gentle whisper in my thoughts.

But would she like it?
She liked it.
We had dinner; this time she left Luigi behind.
And my losing streak?
What losing streak?

13

'Is It Losing?'

Miami, September 1986

The President of Pakistan, Mohammed Zia ul Haq, was speaking to me, 'I wish you and your team the best of luck. Pakistan expects great things from you.'

When the President of your country speaks, you listen; still, as he spoke, I was wondering if he realized that he had just confiscated half of my house.

I was in the strangest position. On the one hand, it was because of the President, a great sports enthusiast, that bridge in Pakistan had finally been given official sanction – a huge step forward for our little band. Since Rye we had been allowed to compete regularly in international events; something almost unheard of a few years ago. On occasion, the players even had government help with expenses.

On the other hand, his government had just ordered the confiscation of half of my house – my brother's half to be exact. With the advent of martial law under Zia ul Haq, my brother had once more found himself in the opposition. And again, he soon had charges made against him for anti-government activities, and this time, rather than spend another period in jail, he had taken political asylum in England. As a result, his property had been ordered to be confiscated: his half of the house we jointly owned in Karachi. How you confiscate half a house is as unclear to you and me as it was to the bureaucracy. Fortunately at the time, thanks to the help of a bridge-loving policeman, and in spite of occasional visits by the local constabulary to inspect the inventory, the puzzle was still unsolved and the order had been restricted to a paper one. Perhaps if we did well in Miami, I could ask the President for a favour.

As usual, we weren't well prepared. For the 1986 Olympiad, slightly unusually, countries were permitted to enter several teams. Two of our best players, Masood and Munir, were unable to participate. And our bridge association, in its wisdom, despite my vehement opposition, had seen fit to enter several teams-of-four into the Rosenblum (the Open Team Championship) rather than a fewer number of teams containing six players each.

The association wanted to give our players as much experience as possible. But this was naïve. In as gruelling an event as the Rosenblum, you need six players in a team so that everyone has the chance to rest.

On the encouraging side, our women bridge players were happy. This was the first time they had been allowed to take part. A surprising development considering the strict codes in Muslim countries regarding women.

Our four-man team consisted of Nisar (Chance) and Nishat, in one room, while Fazli and I, playing together for the first time, were in the other. You will remember that we were all members of the original squad in Rye five years earlier.

The Rosenblum is essentially a knockout event and we were knocked out immediately. *Arrivedérci* – well, almost. The format of the tournament did allow one slight chance for a comeback – a one-in-a-thousand shot. Defeated teams were dumped together in the 'Swiss' and here, over 100 teams traded punches for four days until one team emerged to enter the Rosenblum semifinals. With bridge powers like America, Poland, France and Sweden each represented by several strong teams, who would be playing in the Swiss, we didn't have much hope – or did we?

Somehow the magic of Rye repeated itself. Once again our team started to dance through the opposition, team after team, match after match. We were nearly always completely outclassed, but something – maybe the Goddess of Bridge – was constantly by our side. We just couldn't lose. I've never experienced anything like it.

If we needed something unexpected to happen, inevitably, it did. At times, good opponents would go crazy, having ridiculous misunderstandings against us. Once, on a recount, we squeaked through by one imp. If we bid a slam needing three finesses, a break and a favourable lead, we would always get it – and we could almost claim before the opening lead. That's the way it was.

When the smoke cleared at the end of the four days of almost non-stop play from ten in the morning to two or three the next morning, we somehow emerged, bruised and battered, at the top of the pack, eligible to play in the semifinals.

Who says lightning doesn't strike twice? To be fair our team members had played above themselves – 'out of their skins' – but we had needed much more than that, and we had found it. Now there were four teams left, three from the United States and us.

Our players are colourful characters. Add that to the fact that we were 'no-hopers' – the only obstacle standing in the way of mighty America – and you'll understand why all the non-Americans, and even many Americans, were behind us. Players from every corner of the globe came up and wished us luck. The Canadians, long-time friends of ours, handed out tee-shirts with the words 'Paki-Power' printed on them. Everyone wanted to show their support.

We would need it.

Our opponents in the semifinal were the odds-on favourites for the event. A crack team bristling with talent: Ronnie Rubin, Mike Becker, Peter Weischsel, Michael Lawrence and our tormenters from Rye, Jeff Meckstroth and Eric Rodwell – or Meckwell, as they are known.

From the first board, the 64-board match turned out to be a tug of war. The lead swung backwards and forwards. With sixteen boards, one session, to go, the score stood at America 105 Pakistan 127.

Things had been going the Americans' way. Now with only a few boards left, I could feel there was nothing in it.

Fazli and I sat against Meckstroth and Rodwell in the Open Room on Vu-Graph. In an auditorium, a large audience would be able to follow the play as it was relayed through from the playing room. Commentators would keep the audience informed and amused during those periods when the players were thinking.

It all came down to the last three hands – the most exciting I've ever played. We didn't know it at the time, but at this point we were eleven imps behind the US. Play in the Closed Room, where Nisar and Nishat had faced Lawrence and Weichsel, was over and the players had rushed to the Vu-Graph to watch the finish. A commentator asked Weichsel how his results had been. He replied confidently that the Americans had had the best of all three hands; he felt they couldn't lose. The audience, all Pakistani supporters, was quiet, sad that our gallant try was about to fail.

'Board 59,' the commentator called.*

---

*The Open Room started with the last three boards, number 62–4. Therefore, we were playing numbers 59–61 last. This allowed a comparison of results with the Closed Room, which played the hands in the correct sequence, so that the running score was known by the audience. Also, the boards have been rotated to make South the declarer in the Open Room.

Dlr: North
Vul: Love All

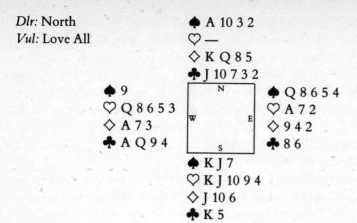

```
            ♠ A 10 3 2
            ♡ —
            ◇ K Q 8 5
            ♣ J 10 7 3 2
♠ 9                         ♠ Q 8 6 5 4
♡ Q 8 6 5 3        N        ♡ A 7 2
◇ A 7 3       W       E     ◇ 9 4 2
♣ A Q 9 4          S        ♣ 8 6
            ♠ K J 7
            ♡ K J 10 9 4
            ◇ J 10 6
            ♣ K 5
```

Open Room:

West	North	East	South
Fazli	Meckstroth	Zia	Rodwell
	1 ◇[1]	Pass	1 ♡
Pass	1 ♠	Pass	2 ♣[2]
Pass	3 ♡[3]	Pass	3NT
Pass	Pass	Pass	

[1] Precision.
[2] Fourth suit forcing.
[3] A splinter bid in hearts!

Closed Room:

West	North	East	South
Weichsel	Nisar	Lawrence	Nishat
	1 ♣	Pass	1 ♡
Pass	1 ♠	Pass	2 ◇[4]
Pass	3 ◇	Pass	3NT
Pass	Pass	Pass	

[4] Fourth suit forcing.

The hand was displayed on the screen, with the bidding from the Closed Room. Our team-mates had bid to the aggressive three-notrump contract.

165

The defence had been quick and deadly. Weichsel, West, had found the precise sequence of plays necessary to defeat the contract. He led the five of hearts, Lawrence winning with the ace and returning the suit: jack, queen. Now Weichsel switched to the four of clubs. Nishat won in the dummy with the ten, led a diamond to the jack, which Weichsel ducked, and then another diamond. Weichsel went in with the ace, and cashed his two club tricks to defeat the game. Nice play.

In our room, Meckstroth and Rodwell were in the same contract. If the Americans made three notrumps, their lead would be overwhelming. Weichsel had read the cards brilliantly – could we do the same?

Fazli also led the five of hearts, and on my heart return won with his queen. He hardly stopped for breath – he led the four of clubs! Plus 50 for East–West. Fazli had found the same defence as Weichsel, almost card for card. (Fazli didn't duck the ace of diamonds for one round.) Cheers shook the building; we were still in the game.

Board 60 came next:

Dlr: East
Vul: North–South

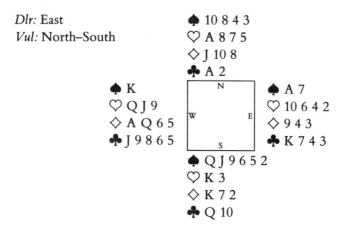

```
                    ♠ 10 8 4 3
                    ♡ A 8 7 5
                    ◇ J 10 8
                    ♣ A 2
        ♠ K            N           ♠ A 7
        ♡ Q J 9                    ♡ 10 6 4 2
        ◇ A Q 6 5   W        E     ◇ 9 4 3
        ♣ J 9 8 6 5               ♣ K 7 4 3
                    S
                    ♠ Q J 9 6 5 2
                    ♡ K 3
                    ◇ K 7 2
                    ♣ Q 10
```

Closed Room:

West	North	East	South
Weichsel	Nisar	Lawrence	Nishat
		Pass	2 ◇¹
Pass	3 ◇²	Pass	3 ♠
Pass	Pass	Pass	

¹ The Multi: either a weak two-bid in a major or a strong two-bid in a minor.
² 'Please bid your major at the three-level.'

Our Closed Room result of three spades one down, minus 100, was normal. Again it didn't look hopeful. If Meckwell and Rodwell could stop in two spades, they would pick up points; and if they got to three spades, there would be no swing.

Open Room:

West	North	East	South
Fazli	Meckstroth	Zia	Rodwell
		Pass	1 ♠
Dble	4 ♠	Dble	Pass
Pass	Pass		

However 'Meckwell' like to bid a lot. Rodwell's one-spade opening was light, but as they play Precision, it was limited to fifteen high-card points.

Fazli's double was a little light too as he didn't have four hearts.

Meckstroth jumped to four spades – the lightest action of all, but, as usual, he was applying the maximum pressure. However, pre-empting in spades usually leaves the opponents with no option but to double. They are unlikely to bid at the five-level when they have had no chance to exchange information about suits.

I did double; and for once I was at least closer to having my values than the rest of the table.

The audience roared with delight. The play was identical in both rooms. Both Wests led the queen of hearts, declarer winning with the king. A heart to the ace, a heart ruff, and the queen of spades followed. The Wests won with the king and switched to a low club. Declarer had to lose one club, two diamond and two spade tricks. Four spades was two down, giving Pakistan nine imps.

With one board to go, we were behind by two imps.

The audience were on the edge of their seats, enthralled. Meanwhile on the screen, the last hand appeared:

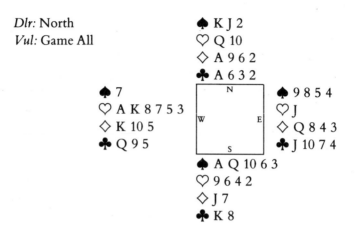

Dlr: North
Vul: Game All

♠ K J 2
♡ Q 10
♢ A 9 6 2
♣ A 6 3 2

♠ 7
♡ A K 8 7 5 3
♢ K 10 5
♣ Q 9 5

♠ 9 8 5 4
♡ J
♢ Q 8 4 3
♣ J 10 7 4

♠ A Q 10 6 3
♡ 9 6 4 2
♢ J 7
♣ K 8

Closed Room:

West	North	East	South
Lawrence	Nishat	Weichsel	Nisar
	1NT[1]	Pass	2♣[2]
2♡	Pass	Pass	2♠
Pass	Pass	Pass	

[1] 12–14 points
[2] Non-forcing Stayman

It looked like it was all over. Nishat and Nisar had, for once, been conservative, stopping in two spades and making four: +170.

The commentator announced that four spades was unbeatable. If Meckwell bid four spades, they would pick up some more points; and if they stayed out of game, we would share the board. Either way, we would lose the match.

The bidding was super-scientific:

Open Room:

West	North	East	South
Zia	Rodwell	Fazli	Meckstroth
	1 ◇	Pass	2 ♠[1]
Pass	4 ♠	Pass	Pass
Pass			

[1] A game-try with five spades and four hearts.

Warned that the heart lead may not be best, I led the five of clubs to the two, ten and king. Meckstroth played a club to the ace, ruffed a club in hand, and exited with a low heart, which I won with the king.

Suddenly, one of the commentators, Michael Rosenberg, noticed something. It was possible, just possible that four spades could be defeated. There was one line of defence, improbable but possible, that would defeat the contract – if only we could find it. Try to spot the killer defence. This was the position West to play:

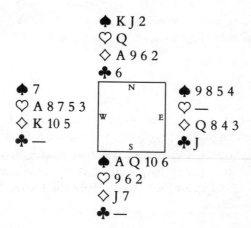

```
              ♠ K J 2
              ♡ Q
              ◇ A 9 6 2
              ♣ 6
  ♠ 7                          ♠ 9 8 5 4
  ♡ A 8 7 5 3      N           ♡ —
  ◇ K 10 5     W       E       ◇ Q 8 4 3
  ♣ —              S           ♣ J
              ♠ A Q 10 6
              ♡ 9 6 2
              ◇ J 7
              ♣ —
```

The winning defence required that I play a trump at this point. When Meckstroth won in the dummy and played a second heart, Fazli had to ruff, even though he would be ruffing a trick that I could win with the ace, to play a second trump. Nothing else would succeed.

The audience shouted me on, willing me to play a trump. (Being quite a way from the auditorium, we couldn't hear.) But when, after a long time-out for thought, I found the trump switch, the audience cheered so loudly that we could actually hear the roar in the room. Meckstroth looked up at me; we both knew the hand must be critical.

It wasn't over. Meckstroth called for the queen of hearts. The spotlight was now on Fazli. Would he ruff? This was real theatre.

Once again he was up to it. He ruffed my trick, and played back a spade! One down, +100 and seven imps to Pakistan. We had beaten the finest team in the world by five imps.

The hotel erupted. Friends, supporters, anyone, everyone rushed out to congratulate us.

Suddenly a voice called out, 'Pakistan zindabad!' Another followed.

The cry was taken up. The sound echoed throughout the hotel as everyone chanted, 'Long live Pakistan!' It was a proud moment.

Unfortunately, there was little time for celebration. The match had finished at three in the morning, and the final would start at ten the next morning. Not nearly enough time to get the rest we badly needed.

On the way up to our rooms, I congratulated Fazli on his play throughout the day, especially over the last three hands.

'You did brilliantly to ruff the heart on the last hand when you knew I had the ace.'

His reply left me stunned: 'How could I know you had the ace, you fool! You didn't lead a heart from the ace-king. I ruffed the trick because I thought Meckstroth had the ace!'

It's five years later, and I'm still not sure whether he was serious or not.

The final was an anti-climax. We had done as much as we were able, and once more our miraculous luck deserted us at the last moment. It was almost as if someone were saying to us, 'I'd like to encourage you, but it really would be too much for you to win.' Here is an example:

Dlr: North
Vul: Game All

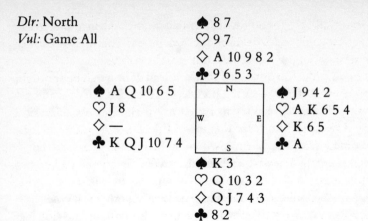

```
                        ♠ 8 7
                        ♡ 9 7
                        ◇ A 10 9 8 2
                        ♣ 9 6 5 3
        ♠ A Q 10 6 5         N         ♠ J 9 4 2
        ♡ J 8                          ♡ A K 6 5 4
        ◇ —              W       E     ◇ K 6 5
        ♣ K Q J 10 7 4       S         ♣ A
                        ♠ K 3
                        ♡ Q 10 3 2
                        ◇ Q J 7 4 3
                        ♣ 8 2
```

Open Room:

West	North	East	South
Nishat	Silverman	Nisar	Lipsitz
	2 ◇	Dble	Pass
3 ◇	Pass	3 ♡	Pass
3 ♠	Pass	4 ♣	Pass
4 ◇	Pass	4 ♠	Pass
4NT	Pass	5 ♡	Pass
6 ♣	Pass	7 ♣	Pass
Pass	Dble	7 ◇	Pass
7 ♡	Dble	Pass	Pass
Pass			

Closed Room:

West	North	East	South
Woolsey	Fazli	Manfield	Zia
	Pass	2 ◇	Pass
4 ◇	Dble	4NT	Pass
6 ♠	Pass	Pass	Pass

In our room, Ed Manfield's two-diamond opening bid was Flannery, which showed a minimum opening with four spades and five hearts. Kit Woolsey's four-diamond response announced, in principle, slam interest in spades with a singleton heart! Manfield used Roman Key Card Blackwood, and Woolsey jumped to try to describe his void. They had an 'accident' but landed on their feet, winning all thirteen tricks for +1460.

In the Open Room, Neil Silverman had been studying SAPP. His two-diamond opening showed a weak two-bid in hearts, diamonds or clubs, or a weak minor two-suiter, or some strong possibilities. After that a confused auction ensued. Seven clubs would have made, of course, but Silverman found a well-timed double, thinking his ace of diamonds was cashing. Nisar had been trying to get to the right major-suit game, so he tried once more with seven diamonds.

By this time Nishat thought the whole thing was a bad dream – he bid seven hearts, one grand slam they couldn't make.

Seven hearts doubled went two down minus 500 and eighteen imps to the USA. If Nishat had bid seven spades, Silverman would have doubled, but it would have been laydown. We would gave gained fourteen imps: a swing of *thirty-two* imps!

At the time, people suggested that our poor play in the final was due to our exhaustion. I hope I refuted that in the daily bulletin, where I wrote an article in which I mentioned that our opponents had completely outplayed us and thoroughly deserved their win. And I added from my heart:

'Is it really losing when hundreds of people from far-flung corners emotionally will you to win as if you were their own team? We became not just a Pakistan team, but the representative of the rest of the world. Was that losing?'

14

Inside Out and Upside Down

Miami, September 1986

The semifinal was thrilling, but there were other exciting moments too. For example, this must be a candidate for the most amusing hand ever played in a world championship. On the score-card it appeared as one solitary imp to Pakistan, but the actual story is much more complex than the points convey.

This was the hand:

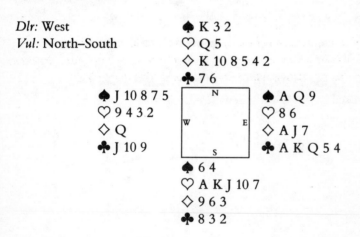

Dlr: West
Vul: North–South

```
              ♠ K 3 2
              ♡ Q 5
              ◇ K 10 8 5 4 2
              ♣ 7 6
♠ J 10 8 7 5           ♠ A Q 9
♡ 9 4 3 2             ♡ 8 6
◇ Q                   ◇ A J 7
♣ J 10 9             ♣ A K Q 5 4
              ♠ 6 4
              ♡ A K J 10 7
              ◇ 9 6 3
              ♣ 8 3 2
```

Open Room:

West	North	East	South
Rubin	Nisar	Becker	Nishat
1♠ ![1]	1NT[2]	Dble[3]	Pass[4]
2♣ [5]	Pass[6]	Pass[7]	2NT[8]
Pass	3◇[9]	Pass[10]	3♡[11]
Pass	Pass	Pass[12]	

[1] The perfect conditions for a psychic one spade.

[2] Either 16–18 balanced or a random hand: but only Chance would bid it at unfavourable vulnerability.

[3] When was the last time your partner opened the bidding, RHO bid one notrump vulnerable and you had twenty points?

[4] Nishat lets his partner do his thing.

[5] Rubin admits to his psych.

[6] Nisar passes – to the relief of the Pakistani supporters.

[7] Knowing that partner has psyched, and worried about his club length, Becker passes. I wish my partners would give me dummies like this.

[8] Not sure what is happening, Nishat keeps the ball rolling.

[9] Nisar is an expert at running – so he runs.

[10] Becker decides that if his opponents have got this far, they must know what they're doing – if only he knew!

[11] Still not sure what Chance is doing, Nishat goes with his 100 honours.

[12] Happy that they didn't get to game!

Nishat was able to win five trump tricks: Pakistan minus 400.

In the Closed Room, sanity prevailed:

West	North	East	South
Fazli	Weichsel	Zia	Lawrence
Pass	Pass	2NT[13]	Pass
3♣	Pass	4 ◇	Pass
3 ♠	Pass	4 ♠	Pass
Pass	Pass		

[13] 20–21 points.

Fazli received a diamond lead. He won in the dummy, and, to keep control, made the fine play of leading the queen of spades. In this way he retained control, driving out the king of spades while dummy could ruff the third round of hearts. We were +420, and a gain of one point for the Pakistan team.

If I told you I picked up a 6–5 distribution, first heard my partner overcall in my six-card suit and then the opponents bid and raise my five-card suit, you might say I was hallucinating. But it was true.

Bridge can be a funny game. Here is the hand:

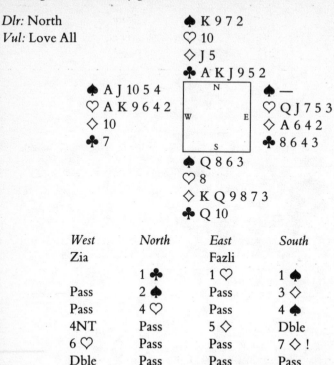

Dlr: North
Vul: Love All

North:
♠ K 9 7 2
♡ 10
◇ J 5
♣ A K J 9 5 2

West:
♠ A J 10 5 4
♡ A K 9 6 4 2
◇ 10
♣ 7

East:
♠ —
♡ Q J 7 5 3
◇ A 6 4 2
♣ 8 6 4 3

South:
♠ Q 8 6 3
♡ 8
◇ K Q 9 8 7 3
♣ Q 10

West	North	East	South
Zia		Fazli	
	1 ♣	1 ♡	1 ♠
Pass	2 ♠	Pass	3 ◇
Pass	4 ♡	Pass	4 ♠
4NT	Pass	5 ◇	Dble
6 ♡	Pass	Pass	7 ◇ !
Dble	Pass	Pass	Pass

Fazli's overcall was light, but you must get into the auction with a distributional hand like that.

Before passing, I checked that both one spade and three diamonds were forcing. Four hearts was a splinter bid, which didn't surprise me.

I knew partner had at most one heart, and has the advantage that in our system four notrumps was always Blackwood. But I was unlucky. South believed my questions and my bidding. I guess I tipped my hand.

We'll draw a veil across our defence. Suffice to say that we got only 300 after I made a stupid club lead.

Almost more amusing than the hand was the fact that the International Bridge Press Association judges conferred on me the Romex Award for my excellent bidding! This was a little ironical as the Romex Award is given by George Rosenkranz, and it was his Mexican team that had beaten us in the first round of the Rosenblum. Naturally I accepted the prize gratefully; but as it's now too late to give it back, I can confess that I wasn't being brilliant in the slightest: I was just thoroughly enjoying myself.

Playing in the semifinals of the Open Pair, we approached a table where two rather serious Continental types were speaking to a lone kibitzer. This was the first hand:

Dlr: South
Vul: Game All

Dummy
♠ A Q 4
♡ Q 9 6 5 3
♢ Q 8 4 2
♣ A

Declarer
♠ K J 2
♡ K 2
♢ A K 10 6
♣ K Q 3 2

West	North	East	South
	Fazli		Zia
			1♢
Pass	1 ♡	Pass	2NT
Pass	3 ♢	Pass	3 ♠
Pass	4 ♣	Pass	4NT
Pass	5 ♡	Pass	6 ♢
Pass	Pass	Pass	

We bid briskly to six diamonds, and West led the four of clubs. If the diamonds broke, the hand would be easy. I led the two of diamonds: nine, king, five.

Typical! The nine forced me to think about a 4–1 diamond break. If West had four diamonds, I would need a friendly lie of the cards. If the diamonds were indeed 4–1, it would be much easier to handle if East were being tricky and had false carded with ♢ J 9 7 3. Then I could simply ruff a club and pick up the trumps.

It was clear that the answer lay in deciding just how good my RHO was: would he play the nine from ♢ J 9 7 3? But how could I determine that? Perhaps I'd get a clue from his convention card. If these guys played something really complicated, I could mark them as experts. No, there were no giveaways. Their names seemed Swedish, so I tried a different approach. 'Do you know P.O. Sundelin?'

No reply. Undeterred, I continued, 'What do you think of upside-down signals?'

He ignored me.

I almost gave him a bidding problem, but rejected the idea. Finally I gave up, if I had never heard of him, he was more likely to be playing an honest card than a devious one. After all, he wasn't Garozzo.

I decided to trust his nine and play for the miracle lie.

Wrong. When I cashed the ace of diamonds, *West* discarded.

East had false-carded – the simple line would have been successful.

This was the full deal:

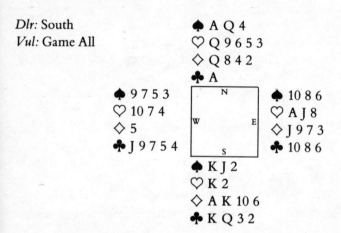

Dlr: South
Vul: Game All

♠ A Q 4
♡ Q 9 6 5 3
♢ Q 8 4 2
♣ A

♠ 9 7 5 3
♡ 10 7 4
♢ 5
♣ J 9 7 5 4

♠ 10 8 6
♡ A J 8
♢ J 9 7 3
♣ 10 8 6

♠ K J 2
♡ K 2
♢ A K 10 6
♣ K Q 3 2

I left the table, furious with myself. But it was only as I walked away that I suddenly realized why I should have known that he must have been a very good player, quite up to an expert false card. What had I overlooked? The kibitzer! He had a kibitzer. In a select field where superstars abound and permission to watch is limited, the spectator had chosen to watch him play over some of the greatest players in the world. He had to be top class.

I missed that – did you?

Returning home after Miami was a new experience. For the first time we were welcomed back, and the government even thought our efforts worthy of recognition, presenting us with medals for achievement in Pakistan bridge. We had come a long way.

15

Would you Like to go
to an Orgy?

The North American Nationals

There are three North American Bridge Championships, commonly
known as Nationals, every year. Each one is an orgy – of bridge. A long
way from the classical music of European bridge events, this is Rock 'n'
Roll, American style. I'll agree that the dress is pretty scruffy: the smarter
ones wear jeans and a tee-shirt. I'll agree that the timings are anti-social:
You play eight to ten hours of bridge a day, and eating hours are
unnatural. I'll even agree that the conversation is limited: 'Why did you
lead a spade?' 'How could you play a heart?'

But you'll have to admit that the level of competition is the highest in
the world, and the atmosphere and experience irresistible. And all are
welcome; novices, seniors, even insomniacs are sure to find a suitable
game. And if you think you can handle it, you can match wits against the
best.

Bridge is the only sport where a beginner can play against an expert.
Could you imagine entering a golf tournament with Nick Faldo or Jack
Nicklaus? Or playing a set of tennis against Ivan Lendl or John McEnroe?
And for an entrance fee of only $20–$30 (£12–£18) per day. There are no
money prizes. The reward is pure – the pleasure of playing. Well,
almost. If you're lucky or good enough to win, collecting one of the
major national team titles also qualifies your team for the play-offs to
select the United States national team. The trials winners usually end up
as world champions. Just how long does it take to become a World
Champion? Would you believe only one year? Impossible, you think?

It happened to Seymon Deutsch.

Seymon Deutsch is your everyday guy; your everyday Texas billion-
aire guy, that is, together with cowboy boots and private jet. (Don't sit
in it: his ex-fighter pilots think they're still in Vietnam.) His college
bridge games were long behind him, until, in August 1987, he was
sitting in his office in Laredo when a man entered unannounced. The

stranger mentioned the word 'insurance' – Seymon promptly threw him out.

Not long after, Deutsch's telephone rang: 'Why did you throw my partner out of your office?' Even after twenty years, the voice of Bobby Wolff was unmistakable. The insurance man had been *the* Bob Hamman – the top-ranked bridge player in the world over the last twenty years, and Wolff's bridge partner.

The incident revived Wolff's friendship with Deutsch, and also Deutsch's interest in bridge. They formed a team of Deutsch, Hamman, Wolff and Jim Jacoby.

The rest is history. They won the Grand National Teams. They added Jeff Meckstroth and Eric Rodwell, and won the US Trials. In October 1988 in Venice, Italy, they beat Austria in the final to win the World Team Olympiad for the first time for the United States.

Not all the entrants in a Nationals, which range between five and ten thousand, depending upon the season of the year, can win a national team title. Most have to learn to live with losing all the time. But some find it harder to accept than others. Take the *Head-Banger*.

The Head-Banger is a well-known player who *really* hates losing. In fact, a bad result blows a fuse. He starts banging his head against the nearest hard object, usually a wall. I'm not sure how that helps him, but he doesn't seem to stop. And to date no one's ever heard him complain of a headache.

Bridge players have no sympathy for such antics, as shown on the occasion when the H-B was pitted against a pair of degenerate gamblers who had made him the subject of a large bet. Ron, gambler number one, had bet Steve, gambler number two, that he could entice the H-B to go into his 'act' during their forthcoming seven-board Swiss team match.

The bet didn't last long. This was what the H-B, sitting East, could see of the first board:

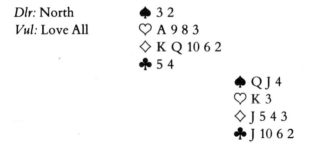

Dlr: North
Vul: Love All

♠ 3 2
♡ A 9 8 3
♢ K Q 10 6 2
♣ 5 4

♠ Q J 4
♡ K 3
♢ J 5 4 3
♣ J 10 6 2

Ron, South, was in six hearts. West, the H-B's partner, led the seven of spades, two, jack, king. Declarer then finessed the queen of hearts, losing to the H-B's king. Back came a low spade, which declarer *ruffed*.

Convinced his partner had underled the ace of spades and handed his opponent with a slam, the H-B couldn't stand it and started to bang his head against the table. Gambler number one promptly stood up and whistled to gambler number two, pointing out that the H-B was banging his head. Steve saw this and reluctantly sent his losses across to Ron via one of the caddies. Once the money had arrived, Ron sat down and said, 'Oh, you led a spade. I'm sorry, I've revoked.' He promptly replaced his trump, the revoke not having been established, with the ace of spades!

The 1987 Fall Nationals held at Anaheim, California, was the scene of one of my favourite wins. It was the prestigious Reisinger, and I was part of a team that wouldn't exist in any game except bridge.

Our strange collection consisted of: An American Jew, a black Christian, an Indian Hindu and a Pakistani Muslim.

Where else but bridge?

When someone asked me how we won (as usual, we weren't expected to), I replied, 'With all the Gods rooting for us, how could we lose?'

I feel there is a key here. I'm sure that bridge can show the rest of the world how easy it is to live together, regardless of race, colour, creed or social background. The only thing that interests a bridge player is his opponents' bidding and defensive carding methods. He doesn't care a hoot about anything else.

The Lion of American bridge is undoubtedly Bob Hamman. No mention of the American bridge scene would be complete without one of his hands. The occasion was the 1985 US Trials. The match was neck and neck. Hamman, sitting East, picked up this hand:

♠ A J 9 5 4 3　♡ A K 5　◇ 10 9 2　♣ 2

With both sides vulnerable, he took part in this auction:

West	North	East	South
Wolff	Cohen	Hamman	Bergen
			1 ♣
Pass	1 ♡	2 ♠	3 ◇
4 ♠	Pass	Pass	4NT[1]
Pass	5 ◇	Dble	Pass
Pass	Pass		

[1] Minor-suit take-out.

His partner led the seven of spades, and this was what he could see:

Dlr: North
Vul: Game All

♠ Q 6 2
♡ 10 9 8 7 4 2
◇ J 8 5
♣ 7

　　　　　♠ A J 9 5 4 3
　　　　　♡ A K 5
　　　　　◇ 10 9 2
　　　　　♣ 2

Dummy played low, Hamman put in the jack of spades, and declarer ruffed. Marty Bergen cashed the ace of clubs: eight, seven, two. Next came the three of clubs, ten, five of diamonds. Plan your defence.

This was the full deal:

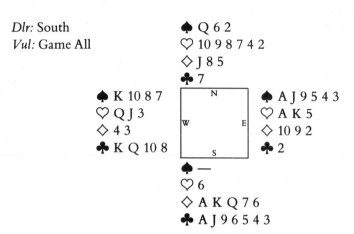

Dlr: South
Vul: Game All

```
                    ♠ Q 6 2
                    ♡ 10 9 8 7 4 2
                    ◇ J 8 5
                    ♣ 7
    ♠ K 10 8 7          N         ♠ A J 9 5 4 3
    ♡ Q J 3                       ♡ A K 5
    ◇ 4 3         W         E     ◇ 10 9 2
    ♣ K Q 10 8        S           ♣ 2
                    ♠ —
                    ♡ 6
                    ◇ A K Q 7 6
                    ♣ A J 9 6 5 4 3
```

Hamman made one of the best defensive plays ever. He *didn't* overruff. His play was so brilliant, I'm not even embarrassed to admit that I wouldn't have even thought of it. Like most people, I would have automatically overruffed and played back a trump. On that defence, declarer would be only one down. But after Hamman's play, the declarer lost control and had to finish three down: a penalty of 800.

In the other room the contract was also five diamonds doubled. However, there West led a trump, which resulted in two down. Hamman's team, therefore, gained seven imps on the board, whereas if he had overruffed, they would have lost seven. The final margin in the match: five imps!

The Nationals are full of weird and wonderful characters, and I've partnered most of them. G— is one of those players who hates to admit to a mistake. Playing with him, he overbid and went for a large number (1100). I had never opened my mouth in the auction and was wondering how he would try to squirm out this time. I found out! G— grabbed his opponent's cards and started screaming, 'How could you double? You had nothing.'

About to play a session with E—, I accidentally brushed against him. There was a hard object near his breast pocket. It wasn't the gun that I suspected, but a carrot on which he nibbled between hands – Bugs Bunny beware.

X— never washes. He smells terrible; so bad in fact that his opponents are always in such a hurry to get away from the table that they don't spend enough time working out their problems, giving X— great results. Who can blame them?

I once approached a table where L—, a black (and obviously gay), was snapping his fingers in time to the tune coming over his walkman. He soon became declarer. In one of my more imaginative moods, I led a fancy queen of spades from ♠ Q 10 3 – disaster. The suit was divided like this:

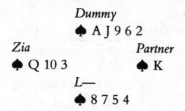

Dummy
♠ A J 9 6 2

Zia
♠ Q 10 3

Partner
♠ K

L—
♠ 8 7 5 4

Naturally I had found the only card to give away the contract. Putting down his radio, L— chortled. 'Don't you know never to lead a black queen gainst a black queen?' It takes all sorts.

The Nationals, together with the New York merry-go-round, were incentive enough. I started to spend more time in America. I took an apartment in the suitably named Trump Tower, and since then, whenever I can get over the jet lag and the occasional losing streak, I've been leading a very happy, if slightly dissolute, life.

And then – there was Atlantic City.

New York is only a few hours' drive from the lights and tournament of Atlantic City.

16

The Man

As we sat down for the final session, I thought of something Somerset Maugham once wrote: 'Bridge is the most intelligent and diverting game that the wit of man has ever devised – I would have children taught it as a matter of course. You can play bridge as long as you can sit up at the table and tell one card from another. In fact when all else fails, bridge remains.'

Yes, but winning would make it that little bit sweeter. To the rest, this was the last day – the end of the tournament. To me it was the beginning. The lessons of Rye and Miami were still fresh in my mind. I knew how easy it was to have nothing left at this stage – and knew I had to avoid that trap.

As the Tournament Director called for silence, I went through my private check list.

1 Wake up.
2 Force my mind into a state of total alertness – aware of every out-of-tempo breath around the table; every change of mood; every kind of feeling.
3 Focus on the ever-changing people around me; who are they?(What do I know about them? Do we speak the same bridge language? How do I get my partner to play his best?
4 Think about the correct way to bid each hand, then go back and recheck. Make sure my reasoning was objective and my analysis not seduced by some flaw in my character.
5 Don't be lazy (my biggest problem) and work hard at even the most simple-looking hands. Appearances can be deceiving. Initial reactions are frequently accurate, but there's no harm in confirming that these impressions were indeed accurate.
6 Try not to let any thing interfere with my mind's ability to work to

its maximum. This is the hardest. It is so easy to be distracted, so human to react emotionally to a disagreeable partner or opponent, or to a disaster, or even to a spectator sitting too close to you.

7 Most of all, think only about winning – nothing less would do.

If I did this on every hand, I would still need to play well and be in luck to beat some of the best minds in the world of bridge. Winning at bridge isn't easy – but that's the challenge.

I was tense and ready for action, but, frustratingly, I had to wait until almost halfway through the session before I had an opportunity to practise what I preach.

Sitting East, I picked up:

♠ 7 ♡ Q 7 3 2 ◇ Q 7 6 2 ♣ A J 5 3

The auction started like this:

West	North	East	South
		Pass	1NT
Pass	2 ♣	Pass	2 ♠
Pass	3 ♠	Pass	4 ♠
Pass	Pass	?	

4–4–4–1 hands are dangerous – with all the suits breaking badly, it's usually right to defend. This one started off unremarkably, but things improved. My rubber-bridge years stood me in good stead.

Everything was ideal. The auction was limited. Trumps were breaking badly, and I needed to get moving. Besides, how many chances would I get?

'Double!'

I struck gold. This was the full deal:

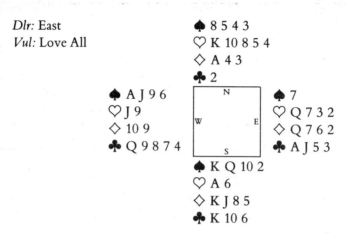

Dlr: East
Vul: Love All

North
♠ 8 5 4 3
♡ K 10 8 5 4
♢ A 4 3
♣ 2

West
♠ A J 9 6
♡ J 9
♢ 10 9
♣ Q 9 8 7 4

East
♠ 7
♡ Q 7 3 2
♢ Q 7 6 2
♣ A J 5 3

South
♠ K Q 10 2
♡ A 6
♢ K J 8 5
♣ K 10 6

The cards lay perfectly – for us. My partner, Charlie Coon, led a club to my ace. I returned a diamond, the jack being finessed successfully. Declarer entered dummy with a heart to the king, then led a trump up, playing his king. Coon ducked smoothly. Encouraged, declarer cashed the king of clubs and ruffed a club. Hopeful, he led another trump. But when I showed out, he wished he hadn't. Coon took two trump tricks, then played clubs. Two down, +300 for East–West. It was a good pick-up.

Not long after, two of the leaders came to my table. This was a crucial round: the result would be doubly important as they were partnered against me. South was the late Peter Pender, at one time a US figure skating champion and subsequently a three-time world bridge champion. North was P.O. Sundelin, my old friend from the *Canberra* TV series. Yesterday he had been sharing the lead with me. Probably there was still nothing between us. My partner was a young woman whom I recognized, but didn't know by name. I needed a break, something to put a little distance between these two and me.

I could never have imagined what followed.

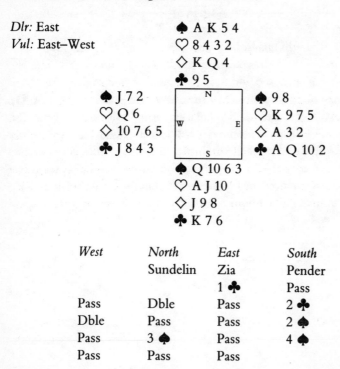

Dlr: East
Vul: East–West

North hand:
♠ A K 5 4
♡ 8 4 3 2
♢ K Q 4
♣ 9 5

West hand:
♠ J 7 2
♡ Q 6
♢ 10 7 6 5
♣ J 8 4 3

East hand:
♠ 9 8
♡ K 9 7 5
♢ A 3 2
♣ A Q 10 2

South hand:
♠ Q 10 6 3
♡ A J 10
♢ J 9 8
♣ K 7 6

West	North Sundelin	East Zia	South Pender
		1 ♣	Pass
Pass	Dble	Pass	2 ♣
Dble	Pass	Pass	2 ♠
Pass	3 ♠	Pass	4 ♠
Pass	Pass	Pass	

North–South did well in the bidding. The game was good but close; there would be plenty of pairs stopping short. It looked bad for us.

Two ladies came to my aid. The first lady was my partner – she doubled two clubs. On the low club lead, Pender played the five from dummy. Knowing from her double that partner had either the king or jack of clubs, I played the queen to keep communication open with my partner.

The second lady was Lady Luck.

Pender, sure that I was about to put up the ace of clubs, played the wrong card – the six instead of the king. When he saw the queen and six of clubs sitting on the table, too late he realized his mistake. I won the trick with the queen, and we took another club trick, a diamond and a heart. Pender had to go one down in his laydown contract. The combination of circumstances was incredible: My closest rival, Sundelin, just *happened* to be his partner. My partner just *happened* to double two clubs (not an obvious action). I just *happened* to play the queen of clubs, not the ace. Pender's concentration just happened to slip for that one second.

Sundelin had watched in horror as his chances of winning disappeared as the six of clubs hit the table. As he left the table he graciously said, 'Forget it, Peter. It could happen to anybody.'

It was likely that this hand had ruined Sundelin's chances, but there were plenty of others in the race. My results continued to be mediocre. Anyone with a big session could overtake me. I needed to do something. I needed to win, as opposed to not losing. But time was running out. By now the pit was surrounded by a large crowd of silent faces. The atmosphere was electric. Sometimes I get a 'feeling' – I got one on this last hand. Perhaps it was because Benito Garozzo – the champion of champions – was my opponent – or that another friend, Pamela Granovetter, was my partner – or perhaps it was just because the vibes were there. I don't know.

Dlr: West
Vul: Game All

♠ A K 6 4 3
♡ J 8 4
♢ A Q J
♣ A 5

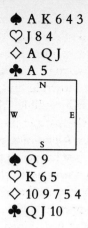

♠ Q 9
♡ K 6 5
♢ 10 9 7 5 4
♣ Q J 10

West	North	East	South
Garozzo	P. Granovetter		Zia
Pass	1 ♠	Pass	1NT
Pass	3NT	Pass	Pass
Pass			

The bidding was simple; Garozzo led the ten of hearts. I called for dummy's four, East flinched slightly before playing the three, and I won with the king. East's 'flinch' told me the hearts were 4–3.

I counted my tricks: three spades (at least), one heart, one club (at least) and four diamonds after giving one up to the king – there was that king of diamonds again. It looked ridiculously easy.

Then why didn't it 'feel right'?

Could anything go wrong?

I went into the 'tank' – isolating myself from everything around me to focus completely on the problem. It seemed natural to play a diamond to the jack. If that lost, I had nine tricks. What if the finesse won? I could either come back to hand with the queen of spades to finesse again, or play the ace and queen of diamonds from the dummy (just in case East was ducking). I always had the spade break to fall back on. I was missing something. I made myself work harder. *What if the diamonds didn't break? What if the spades didn't break? What if both suits didn't break?*

If I finessed successfully in diamonds, and continued with the ace and queen of diamonds, Garozzo would duck his king if he had started with four. Then I would go down if the spades weren't 3–3. There had to be an answer. Suddenly I saw it. The perfect play.

I finessed the queen of diamonds: it won. Then I continued with the *jack* of diamonds without cashing the ace. If it lost, I had nine tricks. If it won and diamonds were 4–1, I could play on spades. It looked odd, even unnatural – it might even cost an overtrick or two. But it felt beautiful, it was beautiful, it was the reason I played bridge. Ninety-nine times out of one hundred it wouldn't make the slightest difference. Today it was the only winning play. Garozzo won the diamond and switched to a club. I won the ace and ended up making five.

The audience was still thinking but my partner, Pamela, knew the play was special. She was the first to congratulate me. 'After that play, you can't lose.' She was right. At that moment I knew I had won.

I was The Man.

This was the full hand:

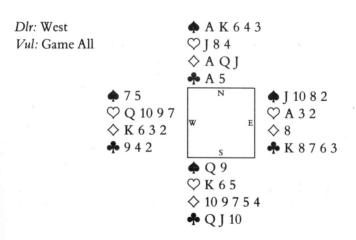

Dlr: West
Vul: Game All

♠ A K 6 4 3
♡ J 8 4
♢ A Q J
♣ A 5

♠ 7 5
♡ Q 10 9 7
♢ K 6 3 2
♣ 9 4 2

♠ J 10 8 2
♡ A 3 2
♢ 8
♣ K 8 7 6 3

♠ Q 9
♡ K 6 5
♢ 10 9 7 5 4
♣ Q J 10

The results confirmed it:

1	Zia	96	Pakistan
2	Fred Hamilton	79	USA
3	P.O. Sundelin	77	Sweden

At the prize-winning banquet, even the Weasel confirmed it. Discussing that last hand, he told me, 'Now that's *one* contract my daughter would not have made.' I couldn't have been paid a greater compliment.

Omar presented the prizes. The casino had a man with a briefcase (just like in the movies) filled with new 100-dollar bills. The winners (maybe they'd lose some of it back) could cash their cheques if they preferred. They preferred!

Tim Holland congratulated me, insisting on buying the champagne.

He smiled and said, 'I can afford it. I won more from Louie than you won in the tournament.' He had played backgammon nonstop for two days.

It transpired that Louie had been losing so much that he suggested increasing the stakes for the last game from the last four digits on the bank note to the last *five* digits. Tim agreed. He won. As they checked the note, the two left-hand digits were nine and eight. 'Keep the change!' said Tim.

We decided to drive back that night, but not before I went to the casino for one last time.

'Don't lose all of your money,' someone shouted.

The casino was almost empty.

'Hey, Zia! What happened to my camels?' For a change, Sarah Jane was at the roulette table. I joined her. The maximum bet on a number was $500. So I gave her $500 and asked for a chip.

'*One* chip'

'Yes.' I placed it on number one. I stood to win $17,000. The ball spun dizzily inside the wheel, then slowing, caressed the one, before it fell close beside it. Thirteen black – you lose. She sounded sad. I smiled.

'*You can't lose when you've already won.* As I walked away, I heard someone ask her, 'Who is that guy? Is he some kind of big-time gambler?'

And her reply:

'No – just a bridge player.'